BAD MUSIC

BAD MUSIC

SUE McCAULEY

Hodder & Stoughton
AUCKLAND LONDON SYDNEY TORONTO

The author gratefully acknowledges the financial
assistance of the Literary Fund of the
Queen Elizabeth II Arts Council of New Zealand.

For permission to reprint previously published extracts in this novel,
acknowledgement is gratefully made to the copyright holders
of 'My Life with Elvis' by Becky Yancey and Cliff Linedecker,
and 'AWopBopALooBopAWopBamBoom' by Nik Cohn.

Editorial services by Michael Gifkins Associates, Auckland.
Typeset by Sharp Image, Auckland.
Printed and bound by Wright & Carman Ltd, Upper Hutt for Hodder
& Stoughton Ltd, View Road, Glenfield, Auckland, New Zealand.

To Keely

one

'He's with a band,' said Sha. 'He sings and that.' And I knew we were in for trouble.

It didn't occur to me to ask if I'd heard of him. I imagined a sharp young man with piebald hair and a disarmingly obtrusive ego. I was warned and I was envious. *Genes*, I thought, thrusting myself into the picture. *I could tell you a thing or two about musicians.*

Instead, I said, 'Oh dear!' and Sha gave her long-suffering smile.

I reminded myself that she must've heard, at one time or another, almost all of my musician stories. Perhaps I told them badly. She had a way of waiting when I got to the end, as if there must be something more — if only to explain why I'd bothered to remember.

My first musician story.

I was eleven years old and the transistor radio had not yet been invented. Our wireless sat in the kitchen high on a shelf of its own. A stretch of dully glittering brown cloth covered its mouth like a polite handkerchief slammed on a sneeze. It was ripped at the lower left-hand corner, and if you stood near the window at a certain angle you could just see the small bright bulb of life within.

The wireless was old and bronchial. Sometimes for hours on end there would be nothing but static. My father would turn the volume knob slowly back and forth. 'Donald Campbell,' he'd say, 'here he comes round the track — he's in the lead now...'

My father listened to rugby matches and the news. The news was BBC — it came all the way from London in a tin tube that ran along ocean floors. The voices came out thin and alien, with oceanic tin-can echoes.

7

Besides rugby matches, news and static, the wireless brought us noise. Noise was Les Paul and Mary Ford. Guy Mitchell, Frank Sinatra, Nat King Cole. Even Edmund Hockeridge — my mother's favourite. *EDMUND HOCKERIDGE*. A name to have you on the floor floppy and insane with laughter.

'Turn off that noise,' my father would say. And we could, without rage or anguish — Les Paul and Mary Ford, I tell you, it was possible to exist without. Their kind of music you could sing for yourself.

On Thursday nights at seven o'clock the makers of bars of washing soap presented the Hit Parade. For half an hour, by special concession, us kids were allowed to listen to noise. There would be eight records, or maybe ten. In the hours before we would each pick our top three. My brother was the best at picking the winners, and my sister was good with tunes, but I was the best at remembering words. Once, in just two listens, I got 'Black-eyed Susie' right through, word perfect.

That was how music was then — a ping-pong tune with words attached. You heard songs in your ears; they came and went like weekends and stubbed toes. All the same I couldn't bear to miss a single Hit Parade, not even in summer when the eels were thick in the creek waiting to be caught. It was as if I knew, even then, that it was all about to change.

Bill Haley came first. They try to make something of that now, but Bill Haley was just Guy Mitchell with an adrenalin rush. An improvement, for sure: not just noise but a jumping-up-and-down-and-grinning noise. My brother got all the words to 'Rock Around the Clock' on his first listen, while I was still stricken with disbelief.

John the Baptist — that was Bill Haley. The little guy who drives up ahead with hazard lights and a sign saying 'Caution — Wide Cataclysm Following'.

It was a wet summer Thursday night of my twelfth year on the planet Earth that the New Zealand Broadcasting Service played on the Hit Parade, first-time-in-at-number-six, 'Heartbreak Hotel'.

Outside it was still daylight. Our kitchen windows looked out across the horse paddock at the encircling hills which seemed, *on rainy days, to swell up and shuffle closer to the house. The kitchen smelt, as always, of mutton fat, but also, this night, of burnt hessian. The pepper and salt shakers and the butter and jam hadn't been cleared from the table. Beside them lay a charred oven cloth; sacking, edged with the floral remnants of my sister's pinafore dress, and made by me at sewing in Standard Four.*

Well since mah-aih babby lerf me . . .

The earth moved. It was the tremor of civilisation rolling over.

I looked at my brother. He was smiling. It was the same smile he used to get when he was winning at cards and didn't want to be smiling but the glee was so huge he couldn't contain it.

My sister wasn't happy, or even looking at us. She had newspaper spread on the floor and was polishing her school shoes. She just stopped rubbing the shoes and stared at the lino, looking vague and troubled.

Our mother came into the kitchen for her cigarettes. She paused with her head held lopsided to listen. 'Good gracious,' she said and went out again.

My brother and I looked at each other. I thought of the story of the Pied Piper, because I knew he and I were both hearing the same thing. And it wasn't just a sound that crashed into our heads and bounced about at number six on the Hit Parade. What we were hearing was in our hearts. It was as if the grey hills had been pushed apart and a vast motorway — a freeway — snaked between them. And at the end of that motorway (promised this voice, this Elvis) *everything was bigger and younger and faster and freer.*

Another country. Where no one need ever polish shoes or go to church or use serviette rings, or even clean their teeth.

Thus it was promised to those of us who believed.

And it came to pass.

When Sha was a toddler she was all rounded and pliable like a puppy. As a baby? I can't remember. Only that I was in a hurry on her behalf; I couldn't wait for her to start talking, get her act together so there would be two of us. But as a toddler she was delectable.

For special occasions I'd tie her hair in a top knot that fountained out like lemon silk. Then it began to turn dark, her hair. Every year a darker shade of brown until last year when it went white with black tiger stripes. I was impressed until she told me how much it had cost.

It was her money. I think she was working, then, in the shoe shop. She'd had seven jobs in the three years since she left school. She didn't know what she wanted to do. That worried me because neither did I. We both knew very definitely that there was some kind of work out there that we would like to do and would be very good at, but we didn't yet know what it was.

When *I* was nineteen you could feel like that and still have prospects. Not any more. These days you have to book into the world before you leave kindergarten. For years I'd been saying to Sha, 'You're good with animals . . . you're smart . . . it'd be great to have an accountant in the family . . . or a mechanic . . .'

As for me, I didn't much expect any more to stumble on a career that was eluding me. I was almost ready to admit that life had, after all, intended me to be an op shop proprietor. Though when I took over the lease four years earlier I'd had no feeling of *coming home*. Scared was all I felt. Worried about breaking even, let alone showing a profit.

We shifted into the rooms behind the shop, and the genteel musty smell of old stored-away clothes was always with us. I used to say to Sha that when the shop was properly up and running there'd be enough work for both of us. A family business like Steptoe and Son. The prospect caused her so much delight she would strangle herself all over our ragged pseudo-Persian carpet.

And conditions were right, heaven knows. As times got harder people began to worry less about *where it had been* and *would it be recognised?* But Second Gear was the right shop at the right time in the wrong place. Right after I took up the lease the young executives started moving into the neighbourhood and the local shops began turning themselves inside-out in an effort to please. Butcher shops became delicatessens and Factory Seconds gave way to unisex hairdressers and BYO restaurants called Georgio's and Anton's.

One by one my regular customers got notice that their rents

were going up in letters soggy with phrases like *I regret* and *of necessity*. And one by one they moved out, to Kingsland, Mt Wellington, Manukau . . . The cranes and the demolition teams moved in.

My lease had two-and-a-bit more years to run. I could go upmarket and turn Second Gear into one of those selective little second-hand boutiques that only buys from *Metro* subscribers. We'd plan that sometimes, me and Sha. *Slumming*, we'd call it. Five changing rooms, each with its own mirror, and a sound system which played Tom Waits and Tracy Chapman. Everything would be painted in a palely tasteful shade of khaki. We'd have to employ a buyer, at least until one of us managed to grasp the fundamentals of good taste. We both found it hard to see beyond our own personal styles — hers being punk rag-bag, mine comfort with big pockets.

But that was just loose talk. As long as there were still some citizens who needed large floral dresses, felt dressing-gowns, worn-in track suits, Second Gear would hang on in there and provide. 'It's not so much a shop,' Clive said, 'as a political statement.' I was ridiculously gratified.

Clive came and went, the way friends do. Two weeks before he'd turned up, back from Canada. He must have been there nearly two years but there was nothing to notice.

'So how was Canada?'

'Okay,' he said.

That's why people feel compelled to travel. It's the only way to find out.

'There was a woman,' he said. 'Vicky. We really liked each other for a while.'

'Yes?'

'I dunno. Yes, I do. I guess I liked her more than she liked me. And my visa had run out, so I came home.'

That's the thing about travel. Disneyland, the Rocky Mountains — they don't really rate when up against the human heart. Except perhaps for India. No one I know has had a love affair in India. Perhaps that's why they all talk about going back there.

'It wouldn't have worked anyway.' Clive licking his wounds.

'Don't go and see *Sid and Nancy*,' I warned him. It was on

at the Academy. Sha and I had been the night before.

'Why not? Might cheer me up. There but for the grace of God...'

'Wasn't like that,' I told him. 'Made me *jealous* for Chrissake?'

'You want to die violently?'

'Passion,' I said. 'Insane ... *annihilating* ... love. It made me feel so grey and...'

'... alive.'

'Only in the literal sense. I suddenly realised my candle isn't burning at *either* end. Not even smoking.'

Clive laughed, and I took the credit. 'Romantic, you'd say?'

'Oh yes.'

'Existential Mills & Boon?'

'I hate smart-arse labels.' I searched for something better. 'It caught a truth. That's the most you can ask from a movie.' I was mildly impressed by the sound of my own mouth. 'In my opinion,' I added. My work had made me humble.

But what had the rest of the audience made of *Sid and Nancy* that night we went? The Academy is a cultured kind of cinema with patrons who wear socks under their sandals. When you walk into the foyer and see them at the tables drinking juice and decaffeinated you think you've blundered into a Christian Youth seminar.

After the movie they walked out silently not looking this way or that, no doubt still trying to blink their way out of that last scene. Sid Vicious and Nancy Spungen dead and victorious. I was crying. I wanted to leap about, celebrate, thank the world for giving us weirdos and people who cared enough to make movies about them. Looking at the people around us. Poker faces. No sign of their having just participated in a glorious uprising against the forces of common sense and moderation. So what were they thinking? *It's only a film?*

Only a film. Only a couple of lives. Only poetry on celluloid. Only hope.

'Ohh...' I moaned to Sha as we hit the bright lights of the foyer, 'I'm envious.'

'Tell me about it!' she said, meaning don't.

'I know! Both of them headcases. All the same...'

Envious. And not just over actor Gary Oldman, with his been-around eyes and universally wicked mouth. I suddenly saw my life stretching ahead in an endless stream of coffee cups and GST returns. Ecstasy = two mallowpuffs for supper, tragedy = irremovable perspiration stains on pastel bri-nylon.

My life wasn't always so stitched up. I was familiar with the sensations back there on the screen, if not the degree. I wanted another turn.

'Shame!' said Sha looking at my red eyes. 'I don't know why I come to these things with you.'

'I'm not crying for them. I'm crying for all mankind. But mainly us old people.'

'There, there,' said my daughter, suspiciously kind, patting me on the arm. When we reached the footpath and turned right she added, 'There's time for me though. For me it's not too late. If I really work at it I could get hooked on drugs and punch people over and throw up in gutters. And then kill myself . . .

'If it would make you proud of me,' she said. Blinking and smirking.

13

two

Looks Don't Count (all that much)
My second musician story

Westshore Beach, Napier. For almost two weeks in the January
of my fourteenth summer my sister and I stayed with our Aunt Elly
and Uncle Roy in a beachside cabin. For secret reasons that were
widely conjectured Aunt Elly and Uncle Roy had no children of
their own. She managed to imply that being childless was the cost
of marrying Uncle Roy. But our mother had a different economic
perspective. Aunty Elly set too high a price on herself to be
burdened with kids, our mother said. (Not once, but whenever the
subject of Aunt Elly arose.)

Aunt Elly didn't want just any old kids. She wanted a daughter.
She wanted the two of them to wear matching mother/daughter
outfits and discuss hairstyles and Cuban heels. My sister said those
were stupid reasons for wanting a child. So what were good reasons?
'The kind our parents had,' said Jan, as if she'd been there.

I asked my mother in the washhouse, 'Why did you have us?'
'God only knows,' she said.

Besides, if Aunt Elly *really* wanted a daughter, said Jan, she could
adopt one. I'd thought of that myself, hopefully, on and off over
the years. It wasn't that we saw a lot of Aunt Elly and Uncle Roy,
they'd lived in London for much of my growing up, but the times
she had visited were embossed in my memory. I didn't especially
like Aunt Elly, but I was enthralled by her trappings. Her earrings
bedazzled me, I was transported by her shoes. Just to look at her
calves in their fine tan stockings, one slung so elegantly against
the other. . . the perfection of her ankles and the charming bridge
of her arches in reinforced nylon.

I was in love with Aunt Elly's clad feet.

*   *   *

'You?' says Sha, in disbelief. 'An admirer of fashion?'

'It must've been just a phase.'

'Get to the musician bit,' says Sha.

They were renting a cabin three doors from ours. Four young men and not an adult in sight. In the afternoons they would travel self-importantly along the dusty road to an old hall where every Friday a movie played. War or cowboys, we'd read the posters. They'd rehearse there for a couple of hours.

In the mornings we'd see them at the dairy buying milk and marmalade — them in jackets and jeans as if they inhabited a different climate, and us with shorts on over our togs because Jan didn't think it proper that people not on the beach should get to see the crease where our legs turned into bottom. Being neighbours and fellow holidaymakers we'd all say hi or at least smile, and I'd be careful to hide my yellow rubber bathing hat beneath my towel.

Jan had a white one. Aunt Elly believed in bathing hats — salt water ruined your hair; she had bought them for us. They felt like a dead person's flesh, and if you held one over your nose it smelt of chloroform.

On the fourth day and the sixth time we'd said hi, one of the musicians said, 'You girls want to hear us play?'

I was still savouring the miracle of this invitation when Jan said no thanks. 'Who do they think we are?' she sniffed as I sulked behind her over the sandhills.

After one swim I manufactured a casual glance between my thighs and a groan.

'I've got my whatsits. I'll have to go and get something.'

'You won't be able to go swimming,' Jan said. She might have been sorry for me but she made it sound like an accusation.

I shrugged, 'I'll have to find something else to do.'

They stopped playing when they saw me inside the hall. They were a Roy Orbison kind of band — basic rhythm and a singer who slid in and out of falsetto. The first musicians I'd ever seen close up. They left Aunt Elly's whole earring collection (thirty-one pairs of studs and twenty-seven drop) for dead.

They were Johnny and the Rockbusters, and on the night of Saturday week they would be playing at the Soundshell. They

15

asked me about Jan. And about Aunt Elly, who'd caught their eye. I told them which part of the beach Jan and I had selected as ours and what times we were usually there. And I'd hardly got back down the beach, saying it must've been a false alarm, must've sat on something, when they all came trooping down to lie on the sand almost next to us and sunbathe in their jeans and denim jackets.

It was all unbelievably fortuitous and quite unlike life as I had come to accept it. So when I realised that the one who seemed to like me was the *singer,* that added leap of extraordinariness seemed totally appropriate.

He was nineteen and five foot eight. He had a pink, fleshy face and sandy hair. His pale freckles were interspersed with a few unfortunate pimples the colour of banana ice-cream. But I had heard him sing. I had seen his lips hover and dip, pollinating the microphone. Already an incredulous voice in my head was recording the details of this momentous relationship.

Aunt Elly approved of boyfriends in that they were a reason for dressing up. But we didn't tell her about the Rockbusters and we tried to look sympathetic when she went on about that dreadful caterwauling down at the hall. Besides, Jan didn't seem to see the Rockbusters as boyfriend material even when they were coming down to our part of the beach every day. Not even when a couple of them peeled off their jeans to let the sun lick at their thighs. She looked at them in the way she'd look at a sandhopper that had strayed onto the open pages of her book.

They were impressed by Jan's indifference and her ability to tackle all those words jammed together in such an unappealing fashion. It would inspire them to awed recollections of brainy people they had met. An uncle who knew poems off by heart, a neighbour's cousin who was a Quiz Kid, a boy in Standard Five who knew the capital cities of every country in the world. I wanted to make it known that I too read books. I wanted Jan to make it known. She never did.

As a romance there wasn't a lot happening between me and Johnny outside of my head. Down on the beach we didn't have conversations. Johnny and the Rockbusters had a line of patter they kept among themselves as if they were rehearsing a comedy routine and Jan and I were the audience. Well, only me really because Jan seldom looked up from her book and sometimes even blocked her ears. But I thought they were wildly funny and original. And I was envious, wanting it to be me lying around with three friends, so used to being together we could pick words out of each other's mouths and blow them up and bat them about.

On the Friday the drummer joined Jan and me in the sea. He was wearing his jeans and a yellow shirt. Even so he could swim better than either of us. He said, looking at me, 'Johnny wants to know if you girls are going to the movies tonight.'

'Depends what's on,' said Jan.

I looked at her.

'It's that cowboy movie — we saw the poster.'

I hated her for that power of being older. I wouldn't be allowed to go on my own.

'We might,' she said.

Aunt Elly's wished-for daughter was the kind who was invited to pyjama parties and had Saturday night dates with tow-headed boys in navy blazers who were allowed to borrow their fathers' cars. She and Aunt Elly would spend all Saturday afternoon getting ready for Saturday night. Setting her hair, shaving her legs and underarms, waiting for the nail polish to dry, choosing the earrings to go with the necklace and the necklace to go with the belt and the belt to go with the shoes. The more I thought about Aunt Elly's daughter the more I didn't care for her.

Aunt Elly blamed our mother. And she blamed our mother's mother, who was Aunt Elly's mother-in-law. 'Brought up like savages,' she hissed at Uncle Roy who pretended not to take it personally. I believed she was mainly referring to Jan: I still took an interest in her earrings and she didn't yet know I'd let the skinny one make paper dolls out of my bathing hat.

'I don't suppose,' Aunt Elly had sighed on our second night, 'either of you get the opportunity to meet any boys.'

'We live with one,' said Jan unnecessarily.

For in a sense Aunt Elly was right. There were the local boys we'd known since primary school and who we now ignored on the tedious bus journey to and from the girls' and boys' high schools in town. There were farm labourers and itinerant shearers, and occasionally an unattached male townie on holiday would be brought along to the swimming hole, or the Tuesday ping-pong. But no tow-headed, blue-jacketed youths to invite us on dates or call our mother Mrs Tunnicliffe or buy us sodas. Aunt Elly understood deprivation.

So we were allowed to fill our days as we pleased while Aunt Elly dragged Uncle Roy around the Napier shops, or they lay on the deck chairs that came with the cabin and read magazines.

'We won't come with you,' Aunt Elly would say to us with unflagging optimism, 'we'd only cramp your style.'

But at tea time the world according to Aunt Elly underwent a sinister change. After tea it was dangerous for us to even walk down to the beach unaccompanied by an adult. On account of larrikins and bad elements.

'Your mother would never forgive me,' Aunt Elly would say, 'if *something* happened.'

The time we spent with Johnny and the Rockbusters — always before tea — felt to me like an achievement. I was sure. . . I was *almost* sure that Aunt Elly would be happily surprised if she walked down the beach and saw us all stretched out on the sand. Jan with her fingers in her ears and a large B for brain embossed on her back in sand glued by a fingersmear of ice-cream. The skinny one making a flute kind of noise by blowing across the mouth of an empty beer bottle. The drummer asleep and the quiet one drawing a ballpoint dinosaur on his own forearm. Johnny dribbling sand softly onto the arch of my upturned foot and smiling whenever I let our eyes meet.

But . . . when we got back to the cabin and Aunty Elly asked if we had a good day and how was the water, we never told her we'd *met some boys*. To be fair to Jan she may not have noticed that Johnny and I were almost going around together. I thought about telling Aunt Elly. I wanted her to know that she could stop worrying, at least about me. But what if she wanted to meet him? Whenever I imagined Aunt Elly and Johnny in social congress I felt an oily undertow in my stomach.

Jan asked if we could go to the movies. It must've seemed, even to her, a better prospect than another evening playing Scrabble or Chinese Checkers with Uncle Roy. Both Aunt Elly and Uncle Roy looked positively relieved. He gave us extra money for ice-creams.

'They could buy a yacht with that,' Aunt Elly said, snatching some of it back.

The movies were an amateur affair with the projector on a table and the audience on old wooden forms. The place was packed long before the projectionist had even opened the box containing the reels. Everyone slow-clapped to hurry him along. The drummer clapped on the off-beat. When the lights were turned off and the numbers on screen counted down from ten, about a hundred hands flew into the projected light and shadow-waved back at their owners.

Johnny was sitting one side of me and Jan the other. He'd bought us both ice-creams. Once the movie had started he found my hand and held it. His hand felt cool and wet like a squashed tomato until I reminded myself that this was the hand of a rock singer.

The Rockbusters were involved in the movie right from the start. They participated in screen conversations, augmented sound effects and suggested alternative courses of action. During the second reel they moved into the space that passed for an aisle, tethered their horses and conducted their part of the shootout crouched behind the water-spout heads and saloon door shoulders of giggling, gawping kids. The skinny one caught a bullet from the double-crossing sheriff and dragged himself through a plantation of jandalled feet writhing and gasping until the drummer tore a strip from the bottom of his own shirt and made a tourniquet to staunch the blood flow.

Eventually Johnny let go my hand and got up to join them. The Rockbusters pointed to him and smiled and waved their fists high. Johnny nodded in acknowledgement and made a small movement from the waist, not quite a bow. Then up, straight and fast, with a gun spinning in each hand and while the watching kids were still smiling he wasted the Rockbusters: one two three.

For a couple of seconds the audience was stunned. The movie ran on unattended. Then a mass of kids heaved towards Johnny, drawing their guns. Trying to keep them steady in that jostle of elbows. The projectionist was yelling for everyone to sit down. Saying he'd stop the movie. No one took much notice, they weren't watching anyway.

Johnny was surrounded. He circled slowly, very deliberately. Then he dropped his guns and inched his hands above his head. The kids relaxed a little. They glanced at each other and grinned. Johnny, eyes down, subdued, moved slowly along our row and sat down in his seat beside me. He crossed his arms and leaned back watching the screen. The kids watched us for a while, I think they felt disappointed, then settled themselves back on the stools. For about a minute there was nothing on the screen but the shadows of heads and bodies scrambling to find places to sit.

On the walk back to the cabins the band talked about Saturday night when they'd be playing at the Soundshell. What if it rained, and how many Hollywood talent scouts were liable to be in Napier on a Saturday night in January? Jan was quite friendly to them. She talked as if we'd be there for sure, so I dared to let myself think about it. The singer's girl. *Me*.

On the Thursday, Jan and I were on the way to the dairy for ice-blocks when Johnny and the drummer pulled up beside us in their old blue van. They were going into town to buy guitar strings and spotted bow ties. Jan didn't want to go. I said I'd meet up with her down the beach. She didn't object.

First we had a good look at the Soundshell. I stood on the stage and bowed and Johnny and the drummer clapped and shouted and yelled, 'More, more!' The drummer bought me a windmill on a stick from a fairground kind of stall in front of the beach. Then we walked through town looking for a music shop and the kind of place that might stock spotted bow ties. We were buying each other things on the way. The drummer would look in a furniture store window and point to a table and say to Johnny, 'I just bought you that table.' And Johnny would say, 'That's the very table I always wanted, thank you, you're a real mate.' Then Johnny would point to a hernia truss in the chemist's and say to me, 'Just a token.'

'You're too kind,' I'd say. 'You spoil me.'

So we were outside a newsagent's shop and Johnny had picked up the triangular billboard sign and was trying to give it to the drummer, and the drummer was saying, 'No, no, I've got one of those,' and Johnny was saying, 'Exactly, it needs a friend. I've heard it crying in the night.' And I was standing with my windmill, giggling, and suddenly at my elbow was Aunt Elly in her green and white spotted sunfrock and her white peep-toe sandals, with her long white teardrop earrings crashing against her neck. Uncle Roy was just behind her clutching a freshly wrapped shoebox and looking nonplussed.

Johnny and the drummer saw them at about the same time. The drummer walked off casually like a passerby. Johnny carefully put the billboard down on the edge of the pavement. With what felt like enormous maturity, I said, 'Aunt Elly and Uncle Roy, this is Johnny of Johnny and the Rockbusters.'

'Pleased to meet y',' said Johnny. He held out a pink hand but they didn't appear to notice. Aunt Elly gave the kind of smile babies give when they're about to throw up and Uncle Roy nodded vaguely as if he was trying to draw attention to the shoebox in his hand.

'We're just on our way home,' said Aunt Elly, clutching me by the wrist and dragging me towards her. I think it was the first time our skins had ever touched, hers and mine.

No one spoke as we drove back to the beach. I sat in the back seat watching the windmill spin in the breeze from my window. I tried to imagine I was cutting up Aunt Elly's sundress to make four unforgettable bow ties.

The next day we packed up and went home because Uncle Roy had developed a war wound headache.

'Yes?'
  'That's it.'
  'Ah.'
  'What did you expect?'
  'Not sure. I just thought maybe there'd be some kind of, you know *point* or something.'

There was going to be but I strayed off it. The point was. . . I think it was . . . that musicians, especially singers — the good ones have a power that defies the logic of market forces. I mean, there's this contemptuous belief that public appreciation is an entirely malleable commodity and talent nothing more than a calculated formula. If this was true none but the young and lovely would get to set foot on a stage. But singers who look like bank tellers or crumpled uncles come up like toadstools and hang on in. Despite the hype and promo merchants sound is still the bottom line. Looks don't count. Van Morrison, Elvis Costello, Meat Loaf, Champion Jack Dupree . . .

'And Johnny?'

'Yes. And Johnny.'

'All *men*,' says Sha. Some agile brainwork and I come up, a bit desperately, with Mama Cass. I know Sha has a point but I don't want to undermine a cheerful theory. *With music, no one is too old, too fat, too short, too black, too white.* It may not be strictly true but I intend to believe it.

A silence while Sha stares at me. 'Thank you,' she says in a desperately sincere voice. 'Thank you for sharing that with me. I feel greatly enriched.' She can't carry it off. Her voice cracks on 'enriched'.

Perhaps I was hoping her musician would be the homely kind. For Sha's sake, I mean. As if indifferent looks would be an antidote to all that superficial stuff of performing. But I've met him now and he's attractive in a grainy fashion. He has one of those long faces favoured by horses and rock stars, furrowed vertically. Hal Barber — even the name seems part of a cliché.

'*The* Hal Barber. Oh, come on, Mum — you must've heard of him.' She was serious.

She brought him into the shop in what I presume was her lunch hour.

'I want you to see the slum I call home. And meet my mother.'

She pushed him towards the counter; he was looking around in genuine interest.

'It may look like St Vincent de Paul,' said Sha, 'but in fact it's the pulsating world of commerce.'

Mrs Sandhu, the only customer in the place, stopped browsing through Girls' Shirts and watched with interest.

'Hello Mum,' said Hal. A mass of teeth there, stained with nicotine. 'I like your place. I really do. What have you got in the way of jackets? I get through a lot.'

'The girls rip them off his back.' She rolled her eyes towards the rafters.

'Yeah,' said Hal, 'bit of a prob actually.'

I wanted to take Sha aside right then and there and say, 'It won't work, love. The last thing anyone needs in life is someone exactly like themselves.'

three

She flips the magazine onto the table in front of me. It's spine-damaged and lies there helplessly.

I see the teeth first; great, craggy herbivorous teeth. We had a horse, us kids, called Tuppence, who bit us all. These could be her teeth menacing the photographer who has jumped, for safety, onto a chair. The camera faces down towards that widespread mouth and the long ravaged face. The eyes are curled up, laughing. He wears his hair long, tied back. (Since then he's had it cut — just long enough for a few half-hearted curls. I'm glad; these days with long-haired males I get to worrying whether it's a preference or, for Godsake, a *statement*.)

He sits at a piano — an ordinary old upright — but his hands are hidden. I turn his face to the table top and flick through pages in search of the cover, the date.

'Year before last.' I can tell Sha is irritated. I reinstate HIM to the centre of my attention. The caption beneath the photo says '. . . *a kind of freedom.*' And the headline is: The Ivory Business.

'It's a way of living,' says Hal Barber. 'I don't know how it compares with other ways of living. I've never been a butcher, say, or an accountant. I'll never get to own a yacht or even a Honda Civic, but there's a kind of freedom. I don't imagine accountants have a lot of fun.'

Hal Barber, pianist/vocalist, is back in his homeland after nine years working the pub/club circuit of Australia and the United States, interspersed with studio work.

Hal left these shores as lead singer with the rock group Belinda's Nightmare (the group split up after eight months in Australia) and has since played with Echo Chamber and

24

the new wave band Dull Thud as well as providing instrumental backing for numerous recording artists.

Back in his homeland with one marriage behind him, Hal is catching up on old friends and hoping to find a 'comfortable' niche in the local music industry.

'No kids,' says Sha, reading my mind.

'Making music is like any skill,' he says. 'The more you do it, the better you get. If you listen to some of the great bands in their earlier years they sound like a pack of uncoordinated roosters. At eighteen you think you've discovered the ultimate sound but in fact you're barely acquainted with the instrument you play. I'm glad I'm finally getting to be an old codger.'

'Thirty-eight,' says Sha. A touch of defiance or possibly accusation. Blaming me for having caused her to grow up in the company of adults? But there was school. She was subjected to her peers for the standard thirty hours a week. I'm thumbing mindlessly through the other pages. *Knit yourself a cotton top . . . Can Fergie stand the strain? . . . You and civil defence . . . Women on scooters.* Sha snatches the magazine away.

'He was also in *Rip It Up* last month. Hah. You're such a snob you know; just because we live in a rathole doesn't mean you're not a snob.'

'Rubbish,' I say. 'I like Fergie. At least she doesn't look inbred.'

But really Sha is angry at herself, I see that. Angry at this compulsion to show him off. Already he invades our living quarters, an invisible gangling presence. I edge past him, uncertain how to handle this. I'm not used to seeing my daughter fragile. Resilience runs in the family. I picture us as tough, me and Sha. Skins like crocodiles. Yet now I feel so anxious for her. Anxious/envious. I write them like that to try to distinguish. An attempt to be objective. Awkward words, both of them. And who knows for sure?

I didn't know he played piano. That's who I'd like to have been — Fats Waller. Fingers dancing above the keys to drop down soft and apparently random as cowpats. Left hand soft-shoe-shuffling, right hand stepping high . . .

He's got a band together for a tour. Not a permanent band.

It's just a way to make a dollar and take advantage of the holiday crowds. At present they are out Thames way staying in someone's house *getting their act together*. (Sha, using just those words, gave me a rueful grin. Because of the cliché or because of what, in her edgy imagination, it might entail?)

He rings her two or three nights a week, very late and never prearranged. Between times the silent phone sits on the kitchen shelf smug in its new and terrible power. Perhaps I exaggerate. It rings often enough. We have friends. Besides, we still get calls for the Oasis Dairy though it's more than three years since they changed the number.

Another musician story keeps coming to mind but I don't inflict it on her.

Hal came, played and was gone again. Off to the far north in his refurbished bus. Their first week's itinerary was given on *CV*, which I watched alone. The Hal Barber Ol' Piano Tour. They opened in the city, at the Gluepot; Thursday, Friday and Saturday night. Sha wanted to go on the Friday night, the two of us.

'Please?' she said.

It was several years since I'd given up those kinds of evenings. I could remember feeling crushed, overheated, fleeced, bored, deafened. I couldn't remember enjoyment. Though there must have been, once upon a time. But: 'Please?'

At the top of the stairs they took our money and stamped the backs of our hands with illegible inscriptions. The posters showed Hal in black and white with his lips clamped tight over a smile. A light cloth cap was perched on the top of his head. Symbolic, maybe. It didn't suit him.

We were an hour or so early, which Sha said was necessary if we hoped to get a table. (I wanted to say clichéd parental things like, 'Surely Hal could arrange for that? Even a complimentary pass? For you, if not for me.) Already the place was packed. The air so full of urgency and longings I felt pain in the back of my throat. I remembered that was another reason I'd stopped coming to these places. All that hope and desperation on parade.

We queued at the bar. A young man in a green striped sweatshirt was staring at me. Whenever I looked back he was watching with pale bug eyes. Eventually he came over, shoving his hand in mine.

'Neville Shelley,' he said. 'Beach Road, New Plymouth.'

'Neville.' My hand flopped up and down in his.

'You didn't recognise me! Guess I was still in short pants those days. Just wanted to say I can still remember your ginger beer.' He seemed so happy and I didn't want to spoil it. I nodded and smiled, trying to look like whoever he thought I was, until the silence began to bother him and he backed off, smiling, into the crowd. Sha had her hand over her mouth and her shoulders were shaking. It was *your ginger beer* that had got to her, I knew.

Even that early there were no empty tables. We found a spot near the stage, sharing with three seriously stoned young men. They fixed us with long thoughtful stares and long mournful smiles. Every so often they turned to one another.

'Man, am I . . .'

'. . . whacked . . . yeah . . .'

'. . . out of it. I reckon . . .'

When does this thing . . . ?'

'Man I am just so . . .'

'. . . yeah out of it, right . . .'

I was concentrating hard on not laughing. I turned in my chair, pretended to be interested in the people behind. I was afraid of catching Sha's eye, her kick or nudge; I was a balloon floating above a bill-spike. Finally I had to leap up and shoulder my way to the toilets. To release what had by then subsided to an overblown snigger. And when I returned the Ol' Piano Tour Band was on stage tuning up.

At high school the music teacher liked me better than anyone else in the class. Without either effort or musical ability I got to be smiled at, talked to, asked for opinions. Why me? At the time I half believed what the other girls told me — she wanted my youthful thighs. Looking back I can see it was my soul she desired; not to possess but to keep company with hers in the wilderness of a provincial Girls' High. She urged me to read Poetry and listen to Good Music. On these matters she was evangelical; without the Arts I would be condemned forever to the bleak deserts of mundanity.

I tried. I had more success with sonnets than sonatas. To me Mozart, Bach, Beethoven were a foreign language, incomprehensible. 'You must persevere,' she told me. 'You must must train your ear, Katherine. The appreciation of Good Music is a privilege that must be earned.'

I failed you, Miss McCutcheon. I didn't train hard enough or long enough. My ear was pig-headed about knowing what it liked. Amazing Rhythm Aces, Joe Cocker, Joan Armatrading, Mink de Ville, Herbs, Carter Family . . . need I go on? The list, Miss McCutcheon, is very long though far from all-inclusive. That range of sound that you dismissed with so much distaste as *pop* has its pearls, its sand, its hollow shells. You might as well disparage Mills & Boon and Penguin in the same breath because they are both paperbacks. Over half the population of the Western world knows this, Miss McCutcheon. And you, a music teacher!

Another thing about my ear: I think it feared the spectre of naked emperors. Besides — though you may not believe this, Miss McCutcheon — Bad Music also enriches the soul.

So why did I stop playing records? When did I tune the Second Gear radio into the National Programme where it had remained mumbling in perpetuity? I was bullying myself over that as I listened to the band play. I was feeling like that shocking moment when you glance into a mirror and find you've turned into your own mother: *how could I have let this happen?*

Without even knowing it I'd given up music — let it go in favour of all the useful things that can be found to fill up the last half of a life. I was watching Hal's fingers skittering across the keyboard and feeling like a desert waterhole catching the first raindrops. I could sense the edges softening on my parched and blistered soul. There were four players but I focused on Hal. He was surrounded by a blue light and I couldn't be sure if it was part of the stage effects or my own grateful hallucination. *I was hungry and you fed me.*

I closed my eyes and felt the music sliding around us soft as water. It was loud, of course. Too loud for logic or resistance. Like a frenzied redemptionist it ordered, begged, threatened, seduced us all . . . lay down dem burdens . . . lift up dem eyes. . . *believe, believe.* We were blessed. We were immersed. We were saved, oh Lord Jesus. I could feel the bass drum thromping in the pulse above my collarbone.

People rose and danced. I longed to join them. I love moving to music — even the absurd coordinated dip and shuffle of ballroom. But my dancing had always embarrassed Sha. It took up too much space. I hadn't mastered the comatose bumble, the pelican knee and ferretty neck of contemporary boogie.

The young man across from Sha rolled his eyes towards the dancers and raised his eyebrows. Then they went off without a word spoken, taking different routes to the space below the stage to dance apart together. I avoided the eyes of the two who were left, in case they would feel obliged to help an old lady onto the dance floor. In that huge jam-packed room hardly anyone looked older than twenty-five. I'd been expecting the bouncer to shuffle up beside me and say, 'I'm afraid I must ask you to leave, you're depressing our regular customers.'

When the band took a break Hal joined us at our table. Two others came with him. I was introduced. Kevin, bass guitar, was lean and brown with one of those fine-boned faces, surprisingly freckled. Long black hair, straight and loose. Beside him Willie looked very young and pale, like some strange Victorian child with a flat moon face and dull disorderly hair. Willie played lead guitar.

Sha was sharing her chair with Hal. I slid across mine to balance on one cheek. Sha's dancing partner was offering his chair to Kevin while he set off to fight his way to the bar. Willie very cautiously lowered himself onto the far edge of my chair. Hal had his arm around Sha.

'She said no way would she come and hear us.'

He was telling me, or maybe Willie who was trying to keep a suitable space between his bottom and mine.

He was looking enormously pleased, was Hal; on his own behalf and for Sha. He took it for granted that she was delighted to be there. Beneath his arm, Sha looked knobbly and fierce like a trapped bird. She was the envy of half the women in that hall, and no doubt a good few men, but she perched there with one eye on the blue yonder.

One of the stoned young men talked music with Hal. He was full of praise. Sha caught my eye with a nudge from hers. That bothered me. It should have been his eyes she was aligning herself with after all those nights of waiting for the phone.

Later I got to dance. First with an altruistic Sha then heedlessly alone. Dancing's a bit like sex — at least so far as I remember; first the ritual movements consciously performed and then the moment when the brain goes into automatic and you and God are arm and arm on a perfect beach on a fine summer night.

The memory, like Count Dracula, dies in daylight. And not remembering makes it easy to abstain. From either or both. There you are — truth is just a sweep of carlight in a dark alley!

It felt a long time since I'd danced like that. When there was music and nothing but music and it caught you up and wove you into the fabric of the sound. And you had no will no needs no thoughts except maybe just an inexplicable optimism about the human race.

four

For a couple of years before Sha started school we shared a house
in Parnell with Miriam and Steve. It was a narrow two-storeyed
house with a poky little backyard and a redeeming grapevine. First
there was just Sha and me and Miriam, who I'd known since the
year I tried Training College. Then the rent went up so Steve moved
into Sha's room and she moved in with me. Steve was a friend of
Miriam's brother-in-law. It seemed easier than advertising.

Steve had dark mermaid eyelashes and a slight lisp. 'Born to be
gay,' whispered Miriam in the kitchen as she filled the teapot. We
fell over ourselves being hospitable at the thought of someone who
would cook and clean and wash dishes. We had it wrong, but he
was nice to Sha. He'd play chasing games on his hands and knees
and let her win at Snap.

Steve worked as a wine waiter in a club and when he was home
Miriam was usually at school. So daytimes there was just me and
Steve and we got comfortable with each other and would talk
endlessly about ourselves. We were both unhappy with our lives;
Steve wanted to be a professional drummer and I wanted to be
someone who knew what it was she wanted out of life. We both
knew where this kind of talk would get us, though we pretended
surprise when it did. And even then we kept our separate rooms
because it didn't seem right to return Sha to her old room like a
garment on appro.

Steve went home to Dargaville in a borrowed ute and brought
back his drums. There wasn't room to set them up but he and Sha
sometimes played bongo rhythms on the small ones. Then he
got in a working band and quit his regular job. It was a
bluegrass/country sort of band; they scratched a living out of playing

to rural audiences who weren't ashamed to like that kind of thing.

They'd drive fifty to a hundred miles north or south to play in ageing wooden halls with streamers tacked to the rafters and nikau palm fronds spread across the walls. They played for twenty-firsts and weddings and Young Farmers' socials, and Playcentre fundraisers and New Year's Eves. Played to grandmothers, bachelor uncles, pre-teens, mums and dads, an occasional toddler, and the teenagers who hung around the door to practise leaving. The smaller the community the wider the range of citizens who turned out. It was men at the doorway end of the hall, women at the other end and kids in the middle. And always supper. Trestle tables squatting beneath mussels, oysters, cold roast pork, pavlovas, trifle, coleslaw, and thin white buttered bread.

On the Friday or Saturday nights when Miriam offered to babysit, Steve would take me with him on the pot-luck adventure of a country gig. It was my job to help carry the dismembered metal joinery and ornate diaphragms that he would assemble into a drum set. Then afterwards, to carry those same pieces out again. In the early hours of those far-flung mornings it always seemed to be raining.

There was usually another band wife or girlfriend who had come along for the ride. While there was music we would dance. During the breaks we would offer praise like orange segments. On the nights, and there were some, when their playing was sour and edgy we were inventive.

A Saturday night in a decaying old hall somewhere near the west coast. The dance, if I remember rightly, was to raise funds for restoration work on that same hall — and because the refurbished hall was to be used in part as a youth centre there were more young people among the audience than was usual. An ominous sign for Steve and company; even cowpoke kids are much too sharp for those ol' down-home songs of hogs and heartbreak.

So they had to work hard at first, throwing out the warm-up waltzes and straight into a few Roger Miller fast foxtrots that the kids could move around to. I could see Steve and Wally the bass player exchanging Christalmightly looks from the start.

But it turned out they couldn't go wrong that night. The music came out meshed and easy and Robert the singer loped along the top like John Wayne in the sunset. After a bit the players, hearing themselves, began grinning and even the young grinned back. One of those nights, as Steve would say, that made it all worthwhile. Later they'd use it as a yardstick, trying to analyse just why it went so right. Wanting to find a formula for luck.

Their second break that evening. Steve had come to sit beside me on one of the old wooden forms that hugged the walls. After a couple of minutes we were joined by a very pretty young woman of about seventeen or eighteen. She came and sat on the floor and she took Steve's hand from his lap and held it in both of hers. She gazed at him. I was invisible. Eventually she said, 'What are we doing afterwards?'

Steve slowly inched his neck around to look at me. I said with the edge of my mouth, 'Don't let me stand in your way.' It felt like I meant it. Steve turned back to the young woman and for a long time they just looked at each other. Then he said, 'Sorry.'

I was never sure if what I felt was relief or disappointment.

Hal and company stayed around for a few days before heading north on the first leg of their tour. Sha smiled to herself in the mornings and borrowed thirty dollars to buy herself some purple tights from the market. Both seemed significant. Hal came and went from our little flat. Sometimes Willie tagged along like an angular shadow. His clothes were either too tight or too short. I thought at first it was a gimmick, some kind of David Byrne reversal effect.

Sha and Hal being so engrossed in each other, Willie would attach himself to me. I tried asking him about himself, steering a delicate course between interested and nosy. He'd respond with totally unrelated information ... the habits of Arctic wolves ... the longest recorded time a human being had spent alone in a dark confined space ... did New Zealand have tundra?

Sha told me Willie was a guitar genius. She was, of course, quoting Hal but already his pronouncements come unsourced, such was their authority. 'I knew you'd take to Willie,' she said, 'he's such a durr.'

'A *what*?'

'A misfit.'

33

Hal asked Sha to go with them on the tour. As a roadie or as his piece of fluff, whichever she preferred. 'Either way,' she said, picking over my fresh Saturday garage-sale stock, 'amounts to the same thing. So it's out of the question.'

I think she was hoping I'd put up some other point of view. It was her own fault that I didn't; she'd never taken kindly to advice. Besides, the thought of her leaving home made my heart falter.

I knew she must. I had this cosy vision of the two of us jogging companionably through life, a couple of gritty spinsters happy enough in each other's company. Fine — until you fast forwarded it another twenty years and there I was frayed and querulous; Sha withdrawn and sourly dutiful. The acrid smell of symbioses as we fed off each other's souls.

Then I would think, should I send her away? Is that *my* responsibility? But how — where were the words? 'Child, you are an adult now; take this sword and magic cloak and . . .' When I thought like that I could see her Coppertone calves stepping out the yellow door of Second Gear and pausing for a wrenching second before they turned towards K Road. And I could see her tiger-striped head bobbing between the heads of strangers past the Designercraft Mall. Then my lumpy old maternal heart would gallop after her and beg her back. *Don't leave me, I don't know how to live alone. I'm afraid of empty rooms and uninvited silences. What am I other than the reflection of your loving scorn?*

It took four days for Sha's proud stand to crumble. 'I mean what's the point in slopping pseudo-Aztec designs on crappy old bits of clay? Is that a way to spend a life? I might just as well be hauling around amplifers.'

I knew my role, now, was to protest. To weigh in on the side of gainful employment, caution, responsibility. A covenant that mothers make with the universe: I hereby promise to do whatever I can to eliminate risk, adventure and excitement from the life of this newborn being. The instinct was so strong I'd done the sigh and headshake before I'd even looked at the options. Work or passion.

No amount of maternal knee-jerk could make me that

Calvinistic. Not even in the heart of a recession.

'Go,' I said. 'Go, of course. It's not such a great job and, hell, you might not fall in love again.'

Me neither?

five

Henry Head was eight years old when his mother took a tube of crimson lipstick and wrote SINNER on the side of the ice-cream freezer in Wardell's foodmarket.

From then on her madness made irregular progress. For months on end she would be no different from any other mother. She would make school lunches and peel potatoes and fold away the washing and there was nothing disquieting about the way she did these things. Then, just when they'd begun to feel reassured, she would prostrate herself before the meter reader or cram her mouth with a whole card full of bias binding.

For almost two years her family pretended it wasn't happening. They didn't discuss it. The children took their lead from their father who put on a good performance of being unperturbed, although at night after tea instead of sitting late at the kitchen table with their mother he now went to the piano that stood at the dark end of the passage, and injected a kind of melancholy rage into 'Yes, sir, that's my baby' and 'Chattanooga Choo Choo.'

One night when he opened the piano lid there, painted selectively on white notes, were the letters S C R O T U M.

Only when she was caught feeding the flames she had started with twigs and paper in the entranceway of the old Methodist church did the family acknowledge they had a problem. In court on a charge of attempted arson Mrs Head explained that she'd been acting on instructions from a Shining Voice. From the court she was taken to the hospital at Porirua.

Twice a week Big Barry Head would drive down to visit his wife. He didn't take the children. He told them the hospital knew how to fix their mother up; and when they'd done it he would bring her home. Then one night he packed a small suitcase and said he was going down to be closer to Mrs Head. Just for a few days, he said.

The children waited a week, then another. At this time, Little Barry was nineteen — an apprentice mechanic, Barbara was fifteen and Henry was nine. It was decided that Little Barry and Barbara should take the train to Porirua and find out what was going on. Henry would stay home in case their parents were already on their way back.

Mrs Head was still in hospital. She looked at her two children as if they were a distant view in a foreign country. 'Our father. . .?' they asked her. 'Brian? Your husband — where is he?' She smiled softly and unwrapped another Mintie. They caught the night train home.

After a few weeks as head of the household, Little Barry, who'd always taken after his father, caught the express to Auckland and didn't come back. Barbara and Henry kept this to themselves so as not to be thrown into an orphanage where they would be beaten and starved and made to wear long white gowns. In her last essay for Miss Wilde, the English teacher, Barbara wrote about a sister and brother who were confined in just such an orphanage. She got nine out of ten. *Wonderfully Dickensian, another excellent effort — keep it up. J.W.*

Barbara left school to take a job behind the counter at Adams Bruce. Miss Wilde was appalled and determined to discuss the matter with Barbara's father until Barbara described how her father's pride and fear of ridicule had resulted in such a terrible speech impediment that for an outsider to even attempt to converse with him might cause irreversible trauma. So instead Miss Wilde used her social contacts, and persuaded the editor of the local paper to offer Barbara a trial as cadet reporter.

At school his peers had begun to pick on Henry as soon as word got around that his mother was a loony. They stole his pencils and passed on messages that had no source; they offered him sandwiches with cardboard filling and put maggots in his pencil box. It was Barbara who suggested that when he started at intermediate he should call himself something . . . *a bit sharper* than Henry. It took him three weeks to decide on Hal. It didn't go that well with Head but together they worked out a bunch of Hal and Head jokes so he could get in first.

Barbara graduated from cadet reporter to junior reporter. At work she wrote about flower shows, meetings of the Victoria League, a two-headed foal, the dangers of back-combing, and a family who won the Art Union. At home she wrote poems of great passion and tenderness that not even Hal was allowed to read. They were written for Elvis Presley. She didn't send them. She had no intention of being just another simpering fan. Her love was more complex and more purposeful, and she didn't want to embarrass herself in later life by sending poems that might in retrospect seem second-rate. Her plan was to produce a volume of these poems — to work on them until they were perfect, then find a publisher.

Love Poems
by
Barbara Head

On the flyleaf she would write

> *For Elvis Presley, with deepest affection, respect and appreciation,*
> *Barbara.*
> *(70 Collington St,*
> *Palmerston North*
> *New Zealand)*
> *P.S. If you want to use any of these as lyrics please feel free.*

The rest would be up to him.

She had posters all around her bedroom. Elvis brooding, Elvis grinning, Elvis in leathers, Elvis in baggy-legged suits, Elvis with sideburns, Elvis in khaki and crewcut. Barbara reasoned there were certain things in her favour. Elvis was by now past the peak of his popularity. He was into his recluse phase, holed up in Graceland with a bunch of hoons. The attractions of which must wear off. Obviously he was lonely; still looking for a soulmate among the tinsel and deception called the American Way of Life. Barbara's sincerity, her straightforward no-frills New Zealand kind of love, would speak straight to his saddened heart. There would be no need to include a photo.

When he was home alone, Hal would sometimes take a stool into Barbara's room so that he could turn slowly full circle taking in all those reverberating images. Trying to find a message in the plumped-up lips, the tiny narrow black-fringed eyes.

Then, because he was often home alone, he would take the stool back into the passage and pick out the general shape of a tune on their old piano. There was a sense of relief as he offloaded the burden of sounds which had hung in his head all day. His left hand had an instinct for boogie, his right hand searched for tune. Sometimes when he'd got them both right the piano would dance.

At intermediate Hal was tolerated. At high school he became popular. Long faces were coming into fashion and he was thought to be a wit. He grew rapidly and to save Barbara extra expense he continued to wear a uniform that was several sizes too small. Seen as an act of deliberate defiance, this improved his social status even further.

One morning as the assembled school was about to march into the hall to the military stomp of 'Colonel Bogey', the music teacher suffered a heart tremor. Hal, who was then in the fourth form, volunteered to step into the breach. He sat down at the piano and crashed straight into 'What'd I Say?' His first public performance and it was wonderfully well received until the assistant principal grabbed him from behind in an armlock.

Hal Head; wit, rebel *and* musician.

(Barber came later, when he started to envisage how the name would look on record covers and T-shirts. By then the word *head* had acquired various unfortunate new dimensions. He chose Barber because the word association — Head/Barber — amused him. Also it was a kind of tribute to the memory of his sister.)

The assistant editor, Colin Peterson, was in love with Hal's sister. He was an older man. He had children almost as old as Barbara but they lived with their mother in Ohakune. He wanted to take care of Barbara, to make her life safe and secure. Just as he'd done for his ex-wife up until her departure. He thought the editor gave Barbara too much work and responsibility. He said she should object.

Barbara no longer went to pet shows and Victoria League meetings. She had moved up the ladder to fashion parades and Arbor Day plantings, and culverts the council was reluctant to fence. Also, from time to time, she interviewed famous people. Selwyn Toogood, Howard Morrison, Yvette Williams, Lonnie Donegan. . . When Elvis's gold Cadillac came to town, it was Barbara who wrote the caption and the two-paragraph story. There were rumours — there were always rumours — that soon it would be He Himself. How long can anyone be content with making soggy movies and playing touch football?

'I'll meet him,' she marvelled to Hal. 'They'll send me down to the press conference. We'll be in the same room. He'll talk to me. Can you believe?'

By then she had sent her perfected collection of love poems off to four publishers and two had said 'We regret. . .' and two hadn't replied, even to her follow-up letters. She wondered aloud to Hal if she ought to just hand Him a typed copy, nicely bound, as she left the press conference room.

Barbara was at the A & P show the day the Press Association announced that He was marrying Priscilla Beaulieu. She was waiting for the judge to decide on the best cross-bred ewe and she idly picked up an early edition of the *Evening Post* that someone had dropped on the grass.

When the doctor confirmed that she was pregnant Barbara saw that now her life was slotting itself into place. She was prepared to accept this as inevitable. Colin repressed a wave of horror at the memory of plastic rattles and the sweetly acrid smell of milky vomit and pretended his delight. They agreed on a registry office wedding, all things considered, then Colin remembered he wasn't actually divorced.

The lawyer said he could cut a few corners, but at the very least it would be a couple of months. Barbara was relieved. Despite her thickening waist, they had agreed she wouldn't move in with Colin until they were man and wife. She didn't feel good about leaving Hal even though he had now left school and was working at Yum Yum Takeaways.

On a Friday night in mid-autumn, three weeks before the wedding day, JB Warton was on at the Palmerston North town hall. He'd been on the hit parades the winter before with a song called 'Hot Tears'. It didn't seem like a lot to tour on but the editor gave Barbara a promotion leaflet that claimed JB Warton was the most exciting sound on the US charts since Chuck Berry. There was a photo of a very black man with very white teeth. The editor had arranged with the promotions man that Barbara would do the interview before the rehearsal at six o'clock.

At six-twenty Barbara was waiting in the empty foyer surrounded by posters of the most exciting sound since Chuck Berry. Her editor called the town hall custodian, who called Barbara to the phone. The promoter, he told her, had just rung to say they were running late and maybe she could see Warton after the show? There'd be a ticket for her at the booking office. So maybe, the editor suggested, she'd like to review the show while she was at it? On the other hand no one would care too much if she'd rather just go home and put her feet up. Over to her, really.

The town hall was more than half full. An Auckland group trying hard to sound like the Shadows played for the first hour and Barbara wondered why she'd bothered to stay. In the interval she had three licorice straps and a glass of orange.

JB Warton was just as black as his photo. He wore a pale grey lounge suit, grey shoes and a yellow tie. This was misleading, it turned out. The man sang sack-cloth-and-shackles kind of music, and two-tone-shoes kind of music and some ripped-leathers kind of music. In an hour and a half he didn't come *near* lounge-suit music. Most of the audience felt cheated. 'Hot Tears' had been Johnny Mathis with a beat and that was what they'd come for. Instead this man was playing music *he* liked, you could tell. He was that arrogant.

Barbara could hear the whispers and feel the dead weight of resentment which slowed their clapping hands . . . *raw and honest music which was wasted on an audience seeking a bland studio sound* . . . she composed in her head, knowing it would be altered. The *Evening Banner* never, never criticised the general public.

Climbing the stairs to the dressing rooms Barbara found herself in a queue of young women and girls. She thought they must be responding to an advertisement for an office girl or cleaner but then one of the backing musicians opened the dressing room door far enough to stick his head out and there was a wild surge forward. The musician hurriedly pulled back and slammed the door. Some of the women sighed, others swore. None of them walked away.

Barbara extracted herself from the queue in a hurry. She pushed her way to the door. Someone pinched her hard on the soft flesh of her inner arm and elbows dug into her side. Reaching the door, she knocked firmly. She was quite upset that the musician . . . *someone* . . . hadn't noticed right away that she wasn't just a groupie. She could feel the resentful eyes scalding her back. 'I'm the reporter,' she said when the door was opened by the same musician. He hurried her in and locked the door behind her.

JB Warton pointed to the bottle of whisky in his hand. 'We're having a little party,' he said. 'Or would you prefer beer?'

Barbara was staring at his fingernails, they were so astonishingly pink. It was an effort to look away. 'Whisky, thanks,' she said in a voice that was quite new to her.

The dressing room was small and crowded. All of JB Warton's backing musicians were there as well as some of the Auckland band and a couple of young women. Barbara and JB sat in a corner on the floor and he answered questions about his family and payola and musical influences and marriage. Then she stopped taking notes and he talked about American interviewers (aggressive) and God (unlikely) and Kennedy (symbolic).

The party went on around them and some of the staircase hopefuls got invited in with JB's permission. The albino drummer was refilling their glasses and he said to JB, 'We can see you're all set up, man, but there's aaa-a bit of a serious imbalance here. You reckon —?' Jabbing his finger at the doorway.

JB spread his hands and the pink fingernails disappeared. 'Try and be a bit selective this time, man.' His right hand turned back and slipped silently over Barbara's left hand, devouring it. She could feel the whisky taking her breath away.

Three of the musicians went out to inspect the goods. Eventually they came back with half a dozen who claimed to be over sixteen. JB gave them a fast lookover then he saw Barbara

42

was watching him. He rolled his eyes. It made him look like a take-off of one of those metal nigger money-boxes that tipped the coins into its own gaping mouth.

All those girls being there made Barbara uneasy. It began to feel somehow risky. She stood up steadily and thanked JB for his time and for his wonderful concert.

'Don't go,' he said, trailing his pink fingers down her neck. 'I've got another week in this country. Stay. Travel with me. Then, if you want, I'll take you back home.'

Barbara gave a small test-laugh in case he was teasing. He just stood there waiting. The whisky made it seem quite rational and simple. Hal would be pleased for her.

She would turn in front of the *Evening Banner* building and wave goodbye to the paper and to Colin and her heart would be drunk with freedom and relief.

Then she remembered the baby. Four-and-a-bit-months, like it or lump it. *JB honey, I'd like you to meet someone else's foetus...*

Decadence Hotel,
Las Vegas.
Dear Colin, I'm afraid I have inadvertently kidnapped our baby...

'I can't,' she said despairingly. 'I only wish I could.' She stood on tiptoe to kiss him on the cheek then she blundered out of the room and down the stairs. At her desk in the corner of a scruffy office full of dark shapes and printed whispers Barbara wrote her review ... *the kind of raw vitality and emotional depth that we are unused to.*

'I wish you'd heard it,' she said to Hal. 'I almost wish you'd gone instead of me.' And she told him about JB Warton's invitation. Hal was the only person she could tell who would absolutely believe something like that could happen to Barbara Head.

Two days before the wedding Barbara disappeared. Her friends said nerves... natural... big occasion. Some others talked about breakdowns and genetic disorders. Hal couldn't believe that he knew no more than anyone else.

The wedding day arrived but not the bride. Colin was

convinced there'd been an accident and called in the police. They established that Barbara had withdrawn her savings, applied for and received a passport, and that Barbara Head (or someone purporting to be her) had flown to Los Angeles on the day of the registry office booking.

'She had friends over there?' the police officer asked Hal.

'Not that I know of.'

'I imagine she'll be in touch.'

'Yes,' said Hal.

But he never heard from her. She walked off a plane onto the soil of a strange land and it opened its vast smiling mouth with its white, white teeth and gobbled her up.

The Salvation Army's missing person service didn't come up with anything. When Hal was in the States he made some enquiries of his own, ringing Wartons and Heads from the phone directory. *Excuse me, I'm sorry to bother you and this is a long shot but...* And asking around among the local musicians. *JB Warton — black guy, kind of bluesy rock singer, had a hit in the sixties?* Some remembered but no one knew what had become of him.

Hal has a Disney daydream in which he arrives on foot at the steps of an old southern mansion and Barbara comes out to greet him. A chubby piccaninny of a child is slung on her hip and another peers at Hal from behind a pillar. Barbara looks happy and pretty and proud. She says, 'I knew you'd find me.' She calls to JB Warton to come and be introduced. 'Honey,' she says, 'this here's my brother Hal.'

JB Warton steps forward with his hand extended. His fingernails are shell pink. He wears well-cut jeans, a short-sleeved shirt, sneakers. He flashes a vast and gleaming white smile at Hal. 'Welcome to our home,' he says with a modest wave towards the pillars. He sounds like John Charles Thomas. His hand is dry and warm. 'Hal,' he says in that softly rumbling voice. 'Hey. I know you! Honey, I've heard this cat play. How come you never told me this man is your brother?'

Barbara's mouth falls open, her eyes go wide as a satellite dish.

six

'. . . alias Henry Head.'

It wasn't a question so Hal didn't answer. He was wearing the motel's peach-coloured towel, and water was trickling off his big ugly feet onto the scrawny carpet. He looked around at the two men in suits and the others — three men and a woman — in those crisply laundered shirts so blue it was like a chunk of midsummer sky had invited itself into Unit 7 of the Little Nevada Motel.

Hal could remember all the rational emotions — anger, contempt, fear — but none of them sprang forward to fill the vacuum in his brain. He just kept staring. Two of this lot were little more than kids; so eager and plumply fresh-faced they wouldn't have looked out of place in a playpen. (Another cliché clanging shut behind him *en route* to the grave.)

'You don't mind if I get dressed?' The thought of the questions he should be asking exhausted him. The futility of it. Drug Squad was written all over the plain-clothes pair — the one with the Rottweiler face was flashing it like a metre-high neon sign. Besides, they wouldn't spare five cops for something pedestrian like robbery or manslaughter.

Well, he wouldn't give them the satisfaction of questions. 'Why are you here, have you a search warrant, what have you found?' In the end those crisp blue shirts were the only answer that could be relied upon; the only answer they needed.

He gathered up his clothes and took them back into the tiny space that housed shower, handbasin and toilet. He closed the door, half expecting an objection, but there was none. He dressed slowly, trying to hold the immediate future at arm's length. He could hear them in there busy as barristers, pulling out drawers, hoisting mattresses. The Drug Squad toughs up from the city in search of the early harvest, bent on showing the local bumpkin bunnies just how mean, how cool REAL cops can be. But the pickings must have been disappointing. All wound up for action and stuck here in a town so hick, so mindblastingly boring. . . It was almost worse than tramping through the bush waiting for a gin-trap to shred your ankle. And there'd be pressure coming through from the top to justify the manpower, the motel bills, the helicopter joyrides. . .

So the posters slapped up across from the bottom pub and in the entrance to the unemployment office must have looked like deliverance. Four musicians, a soundman, maybe even a couple of roadies. A whole glorious busload of sure things. 'Is God on our side or wot?'

Hal calculating what they might have found. In Unit 7, let alone Unit 6. The Piano Tour Band had got into town late the night before. George had gone straight to bed but everyone else had gathered in Unit 7, which belonged for the moment to Willie and Hal. It had been working out that way each night — Cosmo and Kevin making sure they didn't share with Willie, but not so it was obvious. There was nothing wrong with Willie except he was a lateral talker and socially clueless. That is, he was no *fun*.

There was a rerun of *Sapphire and Steel* on TV. No one had bothered to turn the sound up. They'd finished off the beer, lukewarm from the bus ride, had a few smokes and Kevin had come up with the exhausting idea of taking everyone miles out towards the coast to meet his whanau. An all-day jaunt to spare them another day in a truculent country town. Hal had been glad to have a solid excuse, or he might have felt obliged to go in the interests of racial sensitivity. Just wanting to be alone was, these days, precariously close to being politically incorrect. Hal crawled into bed and fell asleep listening to them argue over what time to leave.

Unlikely that they would have cleaned up after themselves. But might Willie possibly have tidied things away before he left this morning? Emptied roaches into the rubbish bin? Pushed the odd plastic bag or misused tobacco pouch into the knife drawer? Cosmo, who found the world too claustrophobic to endure unfortified, would have his stash with him in the pocket nearest his heart. So what had been left? The dusty remains of Willie's West Coast special? Maybe two of the generous handful of ready-rolleds Hal had been given by a nice young couple in Kaitaia? Kevin's scrapings of his souvenir deal from Great Barrier?

Hal stopped the inventory. How come they'd got so casual? Even five years ago some measure of consciousness would have reminded them there was risk. But now the presence of dope was so familiar, so trivial, so almost *old-fashioned* it was impossible to muster up a sense of danger let alone a thrilling whiff of sin.

He hung the towel behind the door and rejoined his visitors. The room looked like a pre-teen pyjama party had run amok. Hal wondered who would be liable for damages, if any. He said nothing. They want you on the defensive — haplessly mouthing threats and accusations. Without that the job lacks piquancy.

When Hal came out they all looked at him. He closed the door behind him. He said nothing. He felt like a mouse that refuses to run. He sensed their impatience nudging him with a vast furry paw and he smiled sweetly while he still had the chance.

From the police car Hal glimpsed his own face in a poster and it seemed a bad omen. He had forgotten how been-around, how *used* he'd got to look without even trying. A good face for his line of work. He looked lived-in and laid-back and every year without any effort or pain this got more so. His face caused teenagers to tolerate him, bank managers to distrust him, students newspapers to promote him and proud home-growers to slip him sample produce. On the road towards the end of summer, every day could be harvest festival.

A small office in the local police station. The Rottweiler pushed a chair towards Hal and sat himself in the desk chair. He swivelled it around to face Hal, lifting his knees up, his feet off the floor like a kid. The other plain-clothes man, with his mass of dark curly hair, his big dark Italian eyes and his pitted, tough Irish face leaned against the wall.

'So,' said Rottweiler. 'Let's do some talking.'

Hal rested his elbows on the arms of the chair and clasped his hands together. He looked at his hands. He looked at the ceiling.

'Well?' said Rottweiler. 'We're waiting. All ears.'

'I don't know what to talk about,' said Hal in a fetchingly girlish voice.

'Don't give us that shit.'

Christ, thought Hal, they never change. They must train these bastards on old movies and TV series. *This is a cop. Hear the cop talk. This cop talks tough. This is another cop. This cop talks nice and friendly. He is the sly cop.*

'Let us in on the joke,' said Rottweiler.

Hal shook his head very slightly. 'Bit over your head.'

He knew as he said it it was a dumb thing. Jabbing sticks at a dog before you've checked that the gate between you is latched. Dumb, dumb, dumb. Rule number one: if you can't be nice be neutral.

The Rottweiler left his chair and went to the window. His chum moved forward and sat down. A classic routine choreographed by *Z Cars*. Spaniel, thought Hal, looking at the big dark eyes. Highly strung. Unpredictable. Dangerously intense.

'Names,' said the Spaniel in a soft voice. 'Just give us names.'

'What names?'

'You know.'

'Whaddaya mean I know?'

'Think about it.'

Hal thought.

'Charlie Mingus. Thelonious Monk. Eric Burdon.'

'Hang on, not so fast. Mingus. M I N G I S?'

'G U S.'

'Address?'

'Don't know offhand.'

The Rottweiler wasn't so dense — he was grinning a bit. Not seeming amused so much as pleased at the Spaniel's ignorance. Hal felt sorry, he preferred the Spaniel.

'Famous musicians,' he said kindly. 'You asked for names.'

He was botching it: now they both hated him. The Spaniel was trying to kill Hal with rods of naked loathing zapped straight from his Eyetie eyes. He must have got his training videos mixed up. Anyway this time it didn't work so he had to fall back on the old clichés.

'We can wait,' he whispered, getting up from his chair. 'We've got all the time in the world.'

Hal wasn't wearing a watch and there was no wall-clock. It felt like something after eleven o'clock. Sha's bus was due in at 11.50 am.

'Look,' he said, 'can we stop fucking around? Am I being charged with something?'

'That's what we're here to sort out.'

'You found something back there?'

'Whadda *you* think?'

'I haven't a clue. But you do realise there were half a dozen people in that motel room last night?'

Panic was seeping in. He'd got this far through life without being convicted for anything more than a couple of driving offences and underage drinking — all within the same year. There had been raids, of course. In his younger days Drug Squad visits had been a way of life. He almost used to pity them, feverishly dredging through mounds of decomposing socks and the ancient contents of contemptible fridges. Like prospectors in the gold rush shifting and sifting as if their lives depended on it. Except the prospectors were at least breathing fresh air.

He was charged once, in Australia, for possession. But after one remand his case seemed to have got lost. Just like that; he hadn't even bribed anybody.

What if this time he's charged? Convicted? Fined — how much for a first offence? In the overview, what harm did it do Mick and Keith? But that was them and those were the sixties. These days a cannabis charge is merely a drag, and boring, though in Hal's case the news media will make of it what they can. Another pathetic old hipster caught with his stash down. When almost the whole population under fifty uses/has used/will use the stuff, to be caught is an act of betrayal. Like getting AIDS when everybody knows about prevention. It may feel like bad luck but people see it as *sabotage*. In short, it's uncool. And Hal has never been less than cool since he stopped being Henry. Hasn't even had to work at it — cool and Hal have always been synonymous.

On the other hand, perhaps the news media wouldn't think he rated more than the standard two lines on the court page? Might not even have heard of Hal Barber. Which would be the greater humiliation — to be publicly embarrassed or to be ignored?

The Rottweiler, back in the chair, gave Hal a tail-wagging smile. 'Relax,' he said. 'Who's talking charges? Did we say charges? I'm not saying we came outa that place empty-handed but no worries. No reason why you shouldn't walk out of here not a worry in the world.' His mouth snapped shut, he pushed his clenched fist into his thighs and leaned towards Hal and his powerful shoulders strained against the seams of his shirt. 'On the other hand, if you want make things hard for all of us...'

Hal closed his eyes and had a word with himself. *You are in New Zealand. This isn't Istanbul or Taiping. This is Kaikohe, a frumpy little Northland town with two pubs, a library, an information centre, a police station.* When he opened his eyes he caught them nodding and sending each other eye signals. Another couple of minutes, he thought, and they'd have been sniffing arses.

'Another joke?' said the Rottweiler. 'Try us — we might enjoy it.'

'Tell me something,' Hal looked from one to the other. 'Just as a matter of interest — is this personal? You knew my real name, so you'd gone to the trouble of checking me out. So? Does someone have a thing about musicians — or just about me? I mean, what's the story here?'

An ostentatious cops-exchange-glances routine; so ham it was positively menacing. The Spaniel took over.

'Hal, you've travelled a bit, right? Seen the world...'

'Not recently.'

'Thailand ... South-east Asia...'

'This has got to be a joke. I went there once, eight ... nine years, like millions of other people. Even the Queen no doubt. Someone sent you an inflight list they found in the Bangkok dump, I s'pose, and a nod's as good as a wink?'

Spaniel smiled and shook his head. 'Hal,' he said as if the two of them were really good friends, 'you weren't unknown to us.'

What was that supposed to mean?

'I'm not unknown to a lot of people,' said Hal. 'I'm a performer for Chrissake. It's my fucking job to be known to people.'

'Yeah, of course,' said the Rottweiler. 'You might be interested to know that my daughter — she follows all that stuff, pop music all that — and she's heard of you and she thinks you're useless. No talent at all, she said. That was just last night, I rang home, you see.' He leaned back in his chair and the seams of his shirt relaxed. He had a great big smile on his face; imparting that piece of information had filled him with pure joy.

The extent of the Rottweiler's satisfaction took Hal's breath away. He concentrated for a few seconds on his lungs; in . . . out . . . in . . . out. In his head a clock ticked significantly. He looked round the room but there was no clock in sight. He looked at the Spaniel. 'Can you tell me the time?'

The Spaniel studied his thick-lensed diver's watch. 'Twenty-five to twelve.'

Sha would be cruising through Kawakawa. Gawping with her city eyes. 'Is this place the end of the earth or wot?' Hal had fifteen minutes to wake up from this frustrating dream. He began to get up from the chair.

'Well, it's been very nice but . . .'

'Not so fast.'

'I'm under arrest? So what are the charges?'

'You'll see them soon enough. They're being typed out.'

'So what are they?'

'Best wait and see.'

The Spaniel had gone to the door, and poked his head out. 'Looks like our typist's gone out to lunch. Shouldn't be too long.'

'I've got an appointment.'

'An appointment!' Rottweiler said. 'Goodness me, you should have said. Who with?'

'An electrician.'

'Perhaps you'd like to give him a call.' He nudged the phone in Hal's direction. Hal stared at it. Call Road Services and leave a message? Perhaps he should? Let the hounds on to her and just hope that she's clean.

But what if she's brought a small celebration gift? Something for them to share after Saturday's show. The champagne you

51

have when you're not having champagne. 'No thanks,' he said. The Rottweiler smiled.

Hal took a deep breath. 'Names, you said. That right? I give you a name I can walk out of here? End of story?'

They smiled at each other. 'If it's on the level,' said Rottweiler.

'I guess there's no good me saying this whole thing's a farce?'

Slow smiles, slow headshakes. Pure *Miami Vice*. A case of almost-life imitating almost-art.

'Okay. But I'm not saying I'm certain, you know. I'm just saying possibly, all things considered, and if I was in your shoes... I'd figure here's someone that could be worth your while.' He had their undivided attention.

The bus was five minutes late. In all that gave Hal eight minutes to stand about the footpath hoping she wouldn't be on it — that at some jumpily intuitive last minute she'd changed her mind. And then, as the bus turned the corner from the main street, he was afraid she wasn't on it and his life was nothing more than a tattered old poster gusting down an empty footpath.

Hal carried her backpack to the Little Nevada which was just around the corner and down a block. He chatted on about the trip to Kevin's whanau that they were missing out on, and the riotous night they'd had at the Waiotemarama Hall. He talked to clothe the silences between them for these seemed indecently tumescent.

Unit 7 wasn't locked. Sha gave a small gasp when he pushed upon the door.

'Jesus,' said Hal, 'looks like we've been busted.'

seven

Last winter my sister and I went back for the 75th anniversary
reunion at our high school. Jan lives in Dunedin and I hadn't seen
her since Mum's funeral three years before. We keep in touch in
a vague and obligatory fashion — cards at Christmas and birthdays,
not much more. At best she and I have only ever rubbed along
in a slightly abrasive way.

The high school reunion wasn't quite the triumphant return I had
envisaged thirty years before, in the days when I had no doubt that
some latent talent would emerge to save me from the shame of social
oblivion.

I wasn't at all keen to go, but Jan put on pressure in the form
of three bullying letters within a couple of months, and I was
reduced to the scatty younger sister who sulked and scowled but
did as she was told. I reread the brochure which promised 'an
occasion of fellowship and renewal' and tried to convince myself
that's all there was to it. Besides, I knew of only three renowned
old girls. One was a National Member of Parliament, another
had once won a bronze medal for backstroke at a Commonwealth
Games twenty-odd years before, and the third was a well-
known Auckland socialite — wife of a multimillionaire property
developer. She frequently featured in women's magazines reclining
on garden furniture in the landscaped paddock she referred to coyly
as 'the back yard'.

None of them were my year.

The MP turned up of course. She made a desperately hearty
speech at the opening wine and cheese. Jan was sulking and grinding
her teeth on the olive stones because *she* wanted to be up there
showing off her success and her American football shoulderpads

with the same ungainly defiance. (I'd warned her that intellectuals didn't count for much in the scheme of things; but academics are like the clergy in their blind conviction that their vocation has relevance to the rest of the world.)

At least they hadn't asked the multimillionaire's wife to speak. Or perhaps they had and she'd declined. In fact she didn't turn up at all which caused widespread disappointment. I imagine she had all the envy she could handle; she didn't need to drag her arse down to the provinces and tout for it like the rest of us.

For truly, that's how it was. Oh, there was fellowship and renewal, no doubt, among the young ones with their infinite possibilities. And among the old dears, who were all achievers simply by having so far dodged death. But my year and Jan's; middle-aged and soul-sour in our disappointments. . . seeking vengeance sweet as snakes. There were the predators and the victims, as in fact there had always been, but now I saw these were just different approaches to the same end.

And which was I?

The self-reproachers — most of them butterballs, their little self-covered belts lost among the soft wallow of upholstered flesh — who apologised and apologised and made wispy jokes of self-denunciation. (Sometimes these would be eventually identified as some gorgeous, lisping, Marilyn Monroe-child I'd scorned and envied.)

'Actually,' I said when asked, 'I have a retail business in Ponsonby.' Said it (I think) offhandedly to butterballs and butterball eaters alike, and it had a solid sound. 'I have a business, yes, and a daughter. No, not a husband, not at the moment.' Silly little laugh (mine). Why am I behaving in this cretinous way, competing ready or not?

The self-aggrandisers wore pastel-coloured linen trousers and pixie footwear. Their pert little breasts nudged from finest merino sweaters. They had careers or husbands-with-careers, they'd popped over to Fiji or Rarotonga for a few days last winter, they'd quit smoking and bought PCs. ('My! I'd said in vacant approval four times before I heard some technological *ingénue* elaborate.)

Typecasting apart, the remarkable thing about school reunions is how few surprises they bring. The unworldly girls have grown

54

up to marry clergymen, the goody-good girls have become teachers — and married other teachers (which explains why education remains so dull). Conventional girls grow into conventional adults. The message of inevitability depressed me. I remembered myself dawdling down those corridors making promises. *One day I'll amount to something.*

Being renowned was how I thought of it. *Fame* seemed less dignified and more presumptuous. Renowned for *what*? had seemed irrelevant. Unfocused, I was, then as always.

Jane Gillam was the glorious exception to the rules. 'You remember me,' she insisted, entombing a scarlet-smeared filtertip in its very own portable mother-of-pearl coffin. 'Of course you do, I took up half the bloody classroom. Hardy in her cardy?'

She must have gone through this with everyone she recognised — exhuming her old humilations because only in the light of them could she truly demonstrate HOW FAR SHE HAD COME. I'd noticed her of course — but not recognised... *never, never* would have recognised — at the opening wine and cheese. She'd looked so thoroughly... *renowned* dammit... even down to that naggingly unplaceable familiarity that goes with a touch of fame. Half a head taller than almost anyone else in the room and wearing high heels. Very high heels. Great legs. Straight leather skirt split to the thigh. That overall Joan Collins look where your heart wants to sneer but your face is floppy with admiration.

Whereas...

The Jane Gillam I had known was a large quiet lump of a girl, hunched so her cardigan hung like a new moon from her back. She had a face as round and pale and individual as a railway plate and straight brown hair, short at the back but longer in front, hanging like two lank curtains over her eyes. She had a friend who was barely five foot and thin with a ferretty face. We called them Laurel and Hardy. Their incongruity together seemed the only memorable thing about them. I tried, but couldn't remember Laurel's real name.

This Jane Gillam was a vet.

'A vet?' I'd have believed public relations, or sharemarket. Even escort service.

'That's right.'

'What about ... hell, I can't remember...?'

'Milly. I don't know. We lost touch. I was hoping she'd be here.'

Jane was never my particular friend. But in this reassemblage of Form CP 3 (Commercial/Professional) 1953 onwards she was the one I wanted to hang out with.

I said, 'Perhaps she'll come this afternoon.'

Jane looked round the room judiciously. 'Not if she's got any sense.'

I laughed, aligning myself with the people who were a cut above this sort of event.

Jane shrugged her white-silked shoulders. 'Guess I should be pleased for her. Must mean she's got better things to do.'

Implying she and I hadn't? I wanted to exempt myself from that, but had no grounds. I'd been wondering why the whole event was making me feel so twitchy and critical and now I thought I saw the reason; I was ashamed of not being too busy (in my career as a renowned person) to spare the time.

At lunch they brought out the wine and I began to feel happier until Miss McCutcheon discovered me. Ancient, she was, but still upright and bright-eyed. She had a prim young man in tow — this lunch we were allowed to bring our 'partner' or a 'friend' and the room was spattered with males who had been carefully scrubbed and groomed for display. Was Miss McCutcheon's young man a nephew? A neighbour? Her lover — could it be? She introduced him simply as David.

'Katherine,' she said clutching my arm, dragging me forward for his inspection, 'was one of the petunias in my onion patch.'

She pushed her face close to mine, her eyes were clear and... *young* amid the thousand little lines of her skin. 'You've kept it up? You've kept on thinking ... looking ... listening...?' She was staring at me with a sort of desperation.

'Yes,' I said. It came out as a schoolgirl mutter, embarrassed and surly, but she didn't seem to notice. Her face scrunched up like a happy dishmop.

'See,' she said to the young man. 'The teacher has the power to enrich or impoverish whole lives.'

He nodded solemnly, impressed. She turned back to me.

'And you go to concerts, my dear?'

It mattered to her. 'Yes,' I said. 'Now and again.'

She squeezed my arm approvingly with her bony old hand. 'No one can take it from you,' she said. 'Bring you joy all your life — a love of good music.'

And I only smiled. Poor old rock and roll, thrice thousand times (at least) betrayed for no better reason than snobbery. Though I relabelled this one kindness: sustaining an old lady's illusions.

After that I wandered off on my own. Hoping, I think, to run into the petunia in some memorial corridor, and try to explain. *Unrenowned is not so bad, you know. Besides, I may have another forty years left. Time, still, to find my* métier.

They'd built another block of classrooms about ten years ago. The old music room had gone. In its place was a stretch of tarmac filled, this day, with gleaming cars. Across the road the roof of the old art room showed rusty peaks above the hedge. When the school began to outgrow its buildings it had bought this old villa with wide verandahs and an overgrown garden. The rooms were used to store the gardener's equipment, the broken desks and chairs awaiting repair, and for art.

The art teacher bemoaned this *banishment* to darkness, antiquated plumbing, makeshift facilities . . . but the art room was the only physical part of the school that gave me pleasure.

Now the house was obviously unused. The gate had fallen off its hinges, the path was hidden by creepers and overgrown shrubs, and the roof of the verandah was giving way under the weight of the wisteria vine. One front window was boarded up. The other looked into an empty room. There was no sign proclaiming high school ownership. No doubt they'd sold the property to help pay for what was still being called the 'new wing'.

A couple of old wooden forms stood in the long grass that was once a front lawn. Those old forms are worth quite a bit. I'm always amazed at how people can leave good things to rot away. I sat down on one of the forms. It was shaded all day by the hedge and I had to find a spot not thick with mould.

There was this smell that I hadn't smelt in thirty years. Acrid but not unpleasant. I think it belonged to a glossy-leafed shrub at the side of the house. Though in fact when you put your nose close to the leaves the smell wasn't there. You had to step back a little. For me it was the art room smell — a kind of introductory offer to the more certain smells of oil paints, linseed and damp clay.

I was absurdly happy to be reunited with the smell. I felt it had been expecting me. I wanted to give it the full treatment — clutch it to my chest then push it away for an arms'-length surveillance. *God, you haven't changed a bit!*

She walked up the steps onto the sagging verandah. Skinny legs like two white tent poles splotched with freckles. I didn't see her until that moment and for some reason it was the legs I saw first. I was looking at the backs of her knees, shapeless as matchsticks and moon-pale beneath the ginger blotches. And I knew it was Lil.

She was wearing summer uniform. Blue and white checked pinafore dress over a white blouse. Being Lil the blouse was less than white and the dress was ill-fitting and pulled at the seams. A few inches of hem had come undone. The raw edge drooped against her thighs. The skirt was way above regulation length (an inch above the floor when kneeling), not from coquetry but indifference. It flared from her skinny pelvis like a rough triangle drawn by a child above her stick-figure legs.

I couldn't take my eyes off her. I felt so happy; if I was, at forty-seven, to have a vision how excellent that it should be Lil and not some yellow-tinted saviour.

Her schoolbag bounced against the steps, then was dropped on the verandah and pushed casually against the wall by a black shoe laced with a strip of maroon elastic. The same piece of maroon elastic which, when I first studied it at length, had been so hysterically, inexplicably hilarious I was sent out of a geography class to pull myself together.

She turned towards me then. Everything as I remembered. The long reddish hair, not quite ginger but not quite auburn either, tied with elastic beneath each ear. The thick-lensed owlish glasses with their clear plastic rims (when the fashion was all for Edna Everage two-tone fishtails). White skin emblazoned with very large freckles. Snub nose. Smart mouth, with the kind of curly lips approved by magazines of the time (neither too large nor too small, puckery, and generally closed).

For Lil was quiet in classes and out of them. Mousy was the impression she gave but she didn't really try to make friends. She came at the beginning of the fifth form when we were all pretty much settled into our particular circles. She left her home town and a small co-ed school to board with her grandmother and go to the Girls' High.

There must have been more to it than that but she didn't tell me. It can't be easy to start new at a school in your fifth form but Lil didn't seem lonely so much as once-removed. As if school and classmates were just a glitch in the system that had to be put up with until life's normal transmission could be resumed.

She was taking the same subjects as I was for School Cert so I got to know her a little. We found the same things funny. When some absurdity struck a chord in my solar plexus I would instinctively glance at Lil but at the same time try not to let her catch my eye for she had enviable self-control and I had none.

On a late summer afternoon the dozen or so of us who were taking art found, when we'd trooped across the road, that we had no teacher. Rather than do something constructive we sat around on the lawn waiting for her. Lil wandered up onto the verandah and leaned against the railing. I was watching her. I was thinking how her drabness seemed deliberate. A plain brown wrapper. That behind the gawky glasses and impatiently tethered hair her face was beautiful. And I was wondering if she knew it. I watched her lean forward so her weight was on her stick arms, her shoulders hunched up knobbly as tennis balls. She was like a puppet, all structure and loose joints.

She didn't look at me. Her puppet body contorted, her face collapsed in anguish, she clutched at the collar of her not-quite-white school blouse and began to sing — about a little white cloud that *cri-i-ieeed.*

We fell silent, staring. Lil writhed and wailed. She snatched at her microphone and dragged it down, pleading with it. She wrenched at the neck of her blouse, popping buttons. She fell down on the old grey boards of the verandah and beat them desolately with her fist.

The art teacher rushed in while Lil was still going. The teacher stopped just inside the gate and watched with us. Though I'd heard the song, I'd never seen Johnny Ray perform. I didn't need to — now he could only be an anticlimax. It never occurred to me, then, to wonder if or where Lil had seen him. This was pre-television. Perhaps at the movies? Perhaps she'd never watched him at all, just the both of them knew a good act when they suffered it.

Of course word got about and after that Lil was coaxed to perform on other teacherless occasions, and two or three times she obliged. She could do 'Cry' as well as 'Little White Cloud'. She could probably do Little Richard or even Elvis Presley but we demanded Johnny Ray. The price of success. Then she seemed to get bored with the whole thing and wouldn't do it any more.

So I sat on that damp form in some disposed-of real estate on the occasion of our high school's 75th anniversary and Lil came back to sing for me. And then I knew why I was at that wretched reunion and why I was feeling so obscurely disappointed. I'd come looking for Lil.

But she, of course, had better things to do.

When I first heard Janis Joplin it was Lil I thought of. If there's one thing that I've learnt in half a lifetime, it's that the special people are few and far between. I have let them drift away so easily, thinking the sky was full of stars when any fool could see it's mostly full of empty spaces.

Where are you now, Lil, and what are you doing?

I am Sha-less. The silence around this place makes me lightheaded and, I fear, neurotically self-absorbed. The first two nights I was in a frenzy of release. I couldn't sleep, my brain was dashing about like a fox terrier. I was thinking reassessment, renovation, expansion, New York, night classes, aerobics, dead friends, meaning of life, haircut, yellow jersey, Sydney, live friends, sex, filo pastry, Willy de Ville, reassessment. . . I was shamefully happy and energised.

Thinking back in search of redeeming factors I couldn't remember a time when Sha had stayed away for more than a couple of days. I carried her home from the hospital when she was the size of a weekend roast and now she's half a head taller than me. She hadn't the stomach for running away; she got carsick and she got homesick. At the age of nine she went on a school exchange trip to Whangarei and was so violently, tearfully ill that her billeting family rang in great distress and asked me to drive up and get her.

The Hal Barber Ol' Piano Tour has another six weeks to run. They'll pass through Auckland in the next few days heading south. She won't come back, not to live, not ever. I knew that the morning she left. I thought, that's how endings usually are — sudden and muddled and unremarked on.

The first time I had a good look at the thing that had caused me three weeks of vomiting . . . eight months of indigestion within and medical condescension without . . . an indeterminate period of varicose veins and piles and eighteen hours of execrable pain, I panicked. I thought she had sucked out my life; stolen it like a wicked fairy. I was afraid that a living death may be the price of giving birth. Then I thought of all the mothers I knew and my fears seemed substantiated.

When Sha went off in the bus with the tinted windows and I went home to Second Gear I remembered that old fear. And I saw that it had never really gone away: all that day I wanted to dance with my customers and open champagne and laugh and shout. *I'm still alive. Look at me. I really am still alive.*

A couple of days and nights and it wore off a bit. Being alive, that is. I started compiling mental lists of friends I should go and visit and suddenly remembered all these things about them I didn't like or couldn't be bothered with. At night I would sneak out to the three square metres of dirt we called a back yard and squint at the sky in the hope of seeing something reassuringly authentic like a moon or stars up there beyond the yellow glow of streetlights. I couldn't remember why I was living in the hard and grimy fury of a city when the land was so full of grass and hills and tinkling rivers.

Yet when I thought of shifting out to the country — tried to picture myself in some little cottage, alone except for a cat or dog — I would remember the *silence*. The terrible, infinite, taunting silence that proves that everything that's going on in the whole world is happening somewhere else. I would be *missing out*.

61

On what, for Godsake? *Who knows? But whatever it is, in the country I'd miss out on it.*

So I pulled myself together. I looked through the movie ads but it was all school holiday kids' stuff. I sorted through my wardrobe and swapped the worst of my clothes for some of the nice foreign gear I'd bought at a Swedish couple's garage sale.

Clive called round. He'd got a job as a school caretaker with a two-bedroomed house provided. Already he was thinking it was a mistake to accept. It was out Manurewa way, yuppie country, and all his friends lived right in town. He drew me a map so I could go and visit.

He was thinking of getting someone in to share the house. Maybe a couple. 'Problem is,' he said, 'I've increasingly come to realise that the world's full of people I'd rather not live with.'

I guess I'd never appreciated how lucky I was with Sha. Sitting across the table from Clive I wondered whether he and I could live together. We'd known each other a long time and I liked him better than almost anyone else I knew. I wondered if the same thing had ever occurred to him. I didn't have thoughts like that when Sha was there. They seemed a trifle desperate. Given a choice I'd rather live with Sha than with Clive.

On Friday when I was just about to close the shop a man in a good suit came in. He had a bit of a stroll around while I checked that my little old unused iron bar was still there behind the counter. There was no way in hell that he was a customer. Then he jogged up to me with a big smile and hand extended. 'Ms Tunnicliffe? May we talk business?'

They wanted me to move. There was two-and-a-bit years to go on my lease but they wanted me out last week if not before. *They* being Crowley Rouse Inc. He being John Hargreaves. He left me a card with his name in black letters, embossed so even the blind would know him. The company was buying or had bought our little building — I was too busy mustering my small-businesswoman defences to hear the finer details.

He was disarmingly pleasant, this John Hargreaves. His proposal was that I should find new premises and they would meet my removal costs, and 'if necessary' subsidise the rent until the lease period had elapsed.

'Within reason,' he added and flashed me a smile that said he could see I was a reasonable kind of woman.

'Oh drat,' I said, 'that rules out Parnell.'

'Well,' he said, not seeing it was a joke. 'That depends.'

'If I went upmarket I won't be able to afford the rent once your subsidy ran out.' Me carefully explaining to him something he could have figured out at kindergarten.

'Get onto some agents,' he said. 'I hate to hurry you but maybe you'll be able to look around in the weekend.'

'Not Saturday — that's my buying day. I go round the garage sales.'

He winced. He didn't need these tacky details.

'We'll also keep an eye out and let you know of anything likely.'

'It must have living quarters,' I said.

'We'll keep that in mind.'

I could insist on something fancy and live graciously for a couple of years, then get out when the lease expired. That thought seemed so explosively cunning I didn't dare examine it until John Hargreaves was safely locked outside.

I tore out the back to tell Sha.

'Hey, guess what?' I yelled at the empty flat before I remembered.

eight

While Hal and Sha were shooting pool in the pub at the far end of the town the rest of the band arrived back at the motel. Within ten minutes two carloads of cops arrived, asked all four of them their names, bundled Willie into the second car and drove off.

After a moment of stunned silence Kevin began to laugh. He pulled a plastic bread-bag of dried foliage, bulging fat as a No. 6 chicken, out of the knapsack beside him and held it up. They all laughed. Their amusement was loud with the relief of not being in Willie's shoes.

The three of them who were left went into Unit 6 and had a smoke to calm them down while they waited for Willie. Or for Hal. They had five hours until they were due to play.

'We should've gone with him,' said George. 'Someone should've.'

'Guess so,' said Cosmo.

No one moved.

At the pub the locals were watching as Hal and Sha played another inept game of pool. Hal wasn't used to playing badly but the harder he tried the worse he got. He thought the audience was willing him to lose to this coxcombed girl who barely knew which end of a cue was which. He could feel himself getting knotted up, angry, hating the whole Godforsaken town with its boredom and sullen poverty.

Sha wanted to leave, to go back to the Little Nevada. Or, better still, Auckland. Already it seemed like a bad idea to have come. This wasn't what she'd had in mind, though she did seem to have a bit of a knack for this game. Whenever she made a good shot the guys at the bar would make sounds of appreciation and Hal's smile would get tighter. No doubt he thought they were on her side, but they weren't; they were against the both of them. They were looking at Hal and Sha the way Kath looked at plum stains on a linen skirt.

Alone, or with the other guys, Hal would have had no problem in a place like this. It was a matter of pride; wherever he went, Hal *got along* with people. They liked him. Being a musician helped, of course. Usually there was someone who'd say, 'Hey, aren't you. . .?' Not here, apparently. Not today. Which didn't augur well for the night to follow. Yet there seemed to be plenty of posters around town. Was it possible that they knew who he was and yet. . .?

Because of Sha! That would be it. She walked in with those silly bloody work boots laced to her skinny ankles, with her hair like a rogue clump of ryegrass in a fresh-mown lawn. Red and black ryegrass, what's more. And what they saw was this Pakeha . . . this show-off city bitch who thinks the sun shines out of her arse. And, because Hal is with her. . .

Worse, Sha was starting to panic. 'Hey, fuckwit,' she'd hissed as she passed him the chalk, 'are we leaving, or did we come here to die?'

He crouched and closed one eye, seeing if the yellow was on.

'Relax, for Godsake. You're giving them hostile vibes.'

'*Vibes?*' Her eyes laughing at him over rows of sharp little teeth. 'Vibes. Wow, man. We talking peace here, man? Well I can dig that.'

Because he'd asked her to come . . . because he seemed to be in love with her, Hal let it go. The yellow ball teetered in the edge of the hole then rolled back.

Sha tossed her cue onto the table, scattering balls. She marched out of the bar, not looking back till she reached the glass doors. She let them slam behind her.

Hal removed the cue. He rolled the remaining balls into the pockets. Then he looked at the men at the bar and gave them a big slow grin that said why-do-we-bother?

A couple of them grinned back at him. Hal felt the relief of being in control again. He could finish his drink and leave with dignity.

But a large man of indeterminate years, his jeans slung so low the crotch was between his knees, was swaggering forward with a hand outstretched, finger extended. 'Hey,' he said, 'you're him, eh? Whatsisname? Don' tell me . . . Hal, right? Hal Barber. Shit, you're on all them posters. Buyyu drink, Hal.' Tucking a vast arm around Hal's shoulders and propelling him forward. 'Wanyu to meet my mates. These are my main men and you know who he is, this guy. . .? Whaswrong with yu? Got eyes in yu bum, don't see what's going on around town? Them posters? This is him, right? Hal, this is. . .'

How could he leave? As he told Sha, this was part of the job. He was *obliged* to stay a while and be the centre of attention. They would come along that night, most of them, bringing their friends.

'And you know what'll really get them? What they'll talk about? They'll say — you see that bastard there? He went to a party with Jimi Hendrix.'

'*Did* you?' squeaked Sha, forgetting she was too disgusted with Hal to even speak to him.

'See,' he said. 'Even you.'

'But did you?'

'Well I was at this party and so was he for a while. Mind you, so were a lot of other people.'

'Did you talk to him?'

'Sometimes I tell people I did. I say we talked about Mick Jagger. That way I kind of kill two birds with one stone.'

'Ha ha.'

'What? Oh yeah. Never thought of that.'

By then it was too late to retrieve the anger she had piled up while hanging about the main street (Broadway, the signposts said. *Broadway*!) waiting for him. The truly humiliating thing was that in this absurd little town she hadn't been able to find her way back to the motel; had forgotten which side-street and even whether it was left or right. The map at the post office didn't show motels and she couldn't possibly ask directions from these insanely hostile people, who not only stared but smirked as if she was some joke from outer space. She'd longed to turn round and yell at them 'Whaddareyou? Whereyubeenallyulife?' but she was too young and too full of potential to die.

      *   *   *

Kevin, George and Cosmo were still sitting around in Unit 6 when Hal and Sha arrived. Kevin and Cosmo were swapping siege stories from the cannabis zone. They told about Willie's capture, including the wonderful bit about Kevin's bag which was *right under their bloody noses.*

'Must be family,' said George. 'Someone died or something.'

'Two hours? To tell him his Mum's snuffed it?'

'Six cops,' reminded Kevin. 'Maybe he's wiped someone out? Willie the gangster.' He laughed to himself.

'You were raided,' said Sha. 'Your rooms were done over this morning.' She was looking at Hal. Had he forgotten? Did it happen so often that it didn't seem worth remarking on?

'Ours was. They musta gone through it when I went to get Sha. You musta noticed if they'd been through. . .'

'Is a bit of a mess,' Cosmo looked around him.

'So what's new?' said George with weary disgust.

Kevin hopped off his bed and began walking around, staring at the clothes on the floor, the newspaper strewn in sections, the ashtray, the empty cups. He was getting excited. 'You're right. The bastards've been here. Wasn't like this when we left.' He jumped up and down and cackled with glee. 'They came too soon. Ooooeeee. Bad luck boys — you blew your arses this time. So near but so far.' He picked up his bulging *white sandwich sliced* plastic bag and swung it around his head. Hal wished he'd gone for maturity rather than talent when he was getting this band together. Apart from anything else he didn't know if he could endure seven weeks of apocalyptic weed stories.

'And no one went with him? Or has been up to see what's going on?' He listened to himself sounding so disapproving.

Kevin and Cosmo looked properly guilty, but George just said, in his reasonable way, 'We thought you should.'

Hal couldn't think of a reply. So he ducked down to take a look at the watch on Sha's wrist and pointed out sharply that they only had three hours to go, Willie was missing and they hadn't even looked at the venue.

'That's what we thought you two must've been doing all this time,' said Cosmo in a drawly voice that was supposed to sound innocent. He was watching Sha for a reaction, Hal noticed.

'So I think the best thing is George goes up and sorts out the Willie business. Okay?' George nodded. 'And Cosmo, you'll need to look at the set-up at the pub and I have to talk to the manager. . .'

'I'll go with George,' said Kevin.

'Thanks, Kev,' said George in his soft calm voice, so it could have been sarcastic, but then maybe not. 'Thanks, Kev, that'll be a great help.'

5.30 pm on a muggy Thursday afternoon. Hal walking up Broadway just a little behind Sha and Cosmo, who were laughing and carrying on. How come she got on so well with a hoon like that? Because they were about the same age?

Cosmo knew about sound systems. At least he was the best available at the time which perhaps wasn't saying a lot. He had an inflated sense of his own importance, but if necessary he could easily be replaced. There was a lot wrong with him. For a start his legs were too long and the hat was an affectation. And those sneakers, padded up so it looked like he was wearing a pair of huge white boxing gloves on his feet . . . That silly walk, too. Like a Mickey Mouse cartoon.

They were going past a clearance warehouse. There were stacks of plastic buckets and racks of padded jackets and a carton of grey blankets spread across the footpath. Sha and Cosmo weaved their way between the goods and the three fat women who were sorting through it as if there had to be something golden and splendid — something totally unnecessary — hidden beneath, or in between. And Hal saw how alike they looked from the back. They could have been brothers, with their tricky little bums and that loopy way of walking as if their feet were lead weights on string.

They were having fun. Cosmo took off his hat and gave it to Sha, who shrugged and offered it to a man in a tartan swannie who was going the other way. So Cosmo, with a roar, grabbed it from her and put it back on his head.

Then Sha looked back at Hal, and she stopped and waited for him to catch up.

Happiness ran a wild thumb up and down the keys of Hal's heart, and a song presented itself:

He said, 'I have melted some hearts in my time, dear.

But to sit next to you, Lord, I shiver and shake
And if I knew love, well, I don't think I'd be here
Asking myself if I've got what it takes.'

He'd caught up with her and was singing into an ear so weighted with decoration it looked like a market stall. Singing just loud enough and sure enough for the desultory late shoppers to take an interest. And Sha was embarrassed and enthralled. He could sense her confusion and it gave him pleasure. Her boots tromped along the footpath in step with his old grey sneakers, but they had lost their significance.

'These days we all play cool, calm and collected
Why, our lips could turn blue, just shooting the breeze.'
But under the frost, well, he thought he detected
A warm blush of red and a touch of her knee.

Hal, singing on Broadway! Smiling at the incredulous kids hanging about the door of the fish 'n' chip shop, emoting to parked cars and crumpled cans in the gutter. He even, briefly, put an arm around Cosmo's shoulders, so full, he was, of love and wonder. But especially wonder — at the amazing, glorious fact that, just when you'd think that surely every song the world needed had been written, someone like John Hiatt could come along and knot up your entrails with a simple country tune and lyrics that were so good you felt, the very first time you heard them, that the guy had reached down into some genetic memory pool, because there was this sense of kinship, of *recognition*.

About Willie: Hal wasn't going to start feeling guilty, because the way it was he'd had no option. If they'd kept Hal there (and who's to say *with certainty* they couldn't or wouldn't?), the night's gig — the whole tour — would have fallen apart. They would all be out of a job. And if he was charged — *when* he was charged — he'd have been done for sure, he had that kind of face.

A fine for a first offence, unless the judge had a fetish about cannabis, or musicians. The sentence didn't matter, the conviction did. He'd be trapped — Hal Barber, troubadour, international performer — in a country populated by insane cops. Besides, he was too old for all that shit.

Hal had a friend in Britain who'd been done for a couple of skinny joints when he was old enough to know better. He was a straightforward man and the whole business filled him with a sense of impatience. Against his lawyer's advice he'd defended himself in court: he stood up and told the truth. Yes, he said, that was his cannabis. He'd been smoking the stuff since he was a teenager — not heavily, just now and again, socially. 'In fact,' he expanded, 'much the same way as many of the police officers and lawyers and members of the public here today would use it. Even, perhaps, yourself, Your Honour. It's a fact, Your Honour. Everyone knows it. SO WHAT ARE WE ALL PRETENDING FOR?'

So moved was the judge by this unprecedented display of honesty he convicted the straightfoward man then and there and fined him three times the going rate.

Hal had no appetite for martyrdom; even thinking about marijuana law reform made him yawn. Besides, how do you set about reversing laws that are based on delusion?

Willie had seemed a safe choice. For a start he was so gormless — three minutes of conversation and those two menacing half-wits would see that the lad was clearly not drug syndicate material.

More important, Willie's father was the very rich and influential Duncan Crowley. Which would be reason enough for any cops indulging in a bit of everyday harassment to start talking hot tea and apologies as soon as they realised. But, if it came to the worst and Willie was charged with possession of whatever bits of vegetable matter all those willing hands had been able to scrape together in the room Hal and Willie had shared, and anything that may have been on Willie's person, then Willie's very rich and influential father would talk to the right people and the charge would be dropped. Or — in the very, very worst (and most unlikely) scenario — Willie's father would see that his son was represented by the sharpest and best lawyer in the country. Which would be as good as having the charge dropped, and possibly no more expensive.

Hal had a pragmatic view of the law. Justice was a commodity like anything else; the more you paid the more you got.

But Willie didn't even tell them about Daddy.

'Why not?' said Hal. They were all back at the Little Nevada.

'None of their business,' said Willie.

'All the same,' said George, buttering toast, 'it wouldn't'a hurt.'

'That's what you think,' Willie mumbled back.

He had solemnly promised to turn up Friday when the judge would be in town. Even so, if George and Kevin hadn't arrived, he suspected they would have shut him away. They'd hated him. They'd kept asking him the same meaningless questions. Who did he know? Contacts? Give us names. *Names, prick, and don't bother tryna get smart. We'll leave you a while to think about it. Even without that tin we found enough shit in that motel room this morning to make you a very unhappy young man. You treat us fair and you'll be sweet. Names — you think about it.*

'Your tin was empty,' said Cosmo.

'*Nearly* empty,' Willie whispered.

'Possession?' Hal asked George.

'Guess so. They wouldn't say. Told us that was between them and Willie.'

'So how much did they find in the motel?' Hal asked Willie.

'I dunno. How much?'

Cosmo grinned at Kevin.

'What are they charging you with?' Hal was trying to stay patient.

'No idea,' mumbled Willie.

'They're supposed to tell you,' said Cosmo.

Kevin laughed. 'Which buttercup did you crawl out from under?' Then, to Willie, 'If I were you I'd get onto that phone and ring your old man's lawyer.'

'I can't,' said Willie. 'I don't even know him. Anyway I had nothing, maybe enough for one smoke was all.'

'Willie,' said Kevin, 'they had your name. This isn't just a let's-go-bring-someone-in-and-bust-his-head thing. If it was they woulda taken me. We all know that. There's something going on, Willie.'

'He's right,' said George. 'Get a lawyer.'

'Nah.' Willie shook his head. 'I'll defend myself.'

'Don't be an egg,' said Hal.

You're not helping yourself at all, William. You'll regret this, believe me. We'll make sure you're gonna be sorry about this . . .

Fear and the haphazard cruelty of fate were making Willie's eyes water. Hal, seeing this, had to remind himself that Willie had begun life with a very large serving of good fortune and was therefore due for some of the other kind. It was fate, and nothing to do with Hal. You look at any life and it was like a slice of hillside, layers of bleak grey granite giving way to smooth ochre clay, always a pattern of contrasts. Just like woodgrain. Inevitable.

'So what's the set-up down there?' George changed the subject.

'Good-size room,' said Hal. 'And a stage.'

'Stage? Thassa relief. Bouncers?'

'Two, they said.'

Willie looked at them in amazement. There he was caught up in a totally pointless tragedy of unknown dimensions and already they had lost interest.

'At one point,' he said into the air, 'I said to them, "I don't suppose you've heard of a bloke called Kafka?" And they got all interested. "Kafka? That a nickname? Foreign eh? Address?" '

Sha was listening. She was sitting so quietly hunched on the floor that he'd forgotten she was there until she laughed.

'So I said, "He's dead — but the point is he wrote books about people like you doing what you're doing to people like me." And this cop said, "Read a lot of books about the drug trade, do you?" '

Sha laughed again. Willie felt encouraged to go on.

'And I suddenly saw that all the time what I thought was just normal smoker's paranoia wasn't paranoia at all. I mean it probably seemed like paranoia but in actual fact it was intuition; in actual fact what's happening out there is the social fabric's going insane.'

nine

There was a time when if you went to Memphis and hung around the gates to Graceland with enough passion and persistence, and you were lucky and sufficiently attractive, someone might eventually invite you in. At the very least you stood a chance of being asked along to the Fairgrounds Amusement Park, or the Rainbow Rollerskating Rink, or one of the Memphis movie theatres in the midnight to dawn hours — these amenities having being hired by Elvis because he was in the mood for skating, or Bogart, or fairground rides.

This was in the late fifties, early sixties. Becky Yancey was an Elvis fan who hung around long enough to make it to the outskirts of the inner circle. Then one night at the amusement park she was summonsed to accompany EP himself on the roller-coaster. On the second lap of the track she threw up on him, but being a gallant Southern boy, he ordered himself a change of clothes and took her back to his place for breakfast.

A realistic young woman, Becky asked for a job at Graceland, and got one — as a secretary. After his death she co-wrote a book about her time with the Presley ménage, called, enticingly, *My Life With Elvis*.

I wish I had known at seventeen that all it took to crash Camelot was patience and a beehive hairdo. I like to think that knowing there was a chance, I would have gone. To have experienced life at Graceland firsthand would have seriously hooked anyone into their own life and times.

When Elvis Presley the truck driver turned into a prince, he bought a mansion called Graceland for $100,000, added a few regal

73

touches like the musically notated gates and blue and gold floodlighting, and he had himself a castle. In which he installed — or at least tolerated — a remarkable range of relations, friends, opportunists and hangers-on. And when he became king by acclamation, this strange group were both his courtiers and his kingdom.

This was a real-life fairytale just when we needed one. It was the stuff of myth and legend. All the regular kings and queens and princes and princesses were as worthy and dull as post-war newsreels. They were too starchy to titillate and too ordinary to amaze. Besides, they were British, and Britain belonged to grown-ups. In the fifties, kids knew in their bones that America was irrepressibly, and perhaps eternally, adolescent.

And Elvis Presley was a thoroughly American king. He was excessive, flashy and full of contradictions. Humble and narcissistic, generous and self-indulgent, accessible and remote. Above all he, too, was eternally adolescent. Given more money than anyone would know what to do with he spent it on his buddies, on cars, on motorbikes, hot rods, dodgem rides . . . As the British writer Nik Cohn put it in his book *AWopBopALooBopAWopBamBoom* (written in 1970 — a lovingly irreverent tribute to those early years before rock 'n' roll got serious): 'Definitely, he was young for his age — collected teddy bears, ate ritual peanut butter and mashed banana sandwiches last thing before he went to sleep each night and loved his mother to the point of ickiness.'

It was after mother Gladys died that Graceland came into its own as a cross between a temple and a circus arena. When Elvis was home, according to Becky, every night was open house. Although the upstairs was off-limits, people wandered happily around the main floor and the basement, drank, played pool, helped themselves to whatever was in the fridge and — some of them — to anything else that took their fancy.

Elvis liked to make people happy. He gave his staff, his staff's wives and friends — and sometimes complete strangers — presents of cash, cars, jewellery. His giving was impulsive and therefore inconsistent, and instead of falling about in gratitude and delight, the recipients tended to make comparisons, feel short-changed, vie for greater attention.

For ten semi-reclusive years he lived like Santa Claus in Graceland. His life was every staunch youth's vision of paradise: fame, wealth, women, mates, junk food, two-way mirrors, sleeping all day and yahooing all night. To make this easier he had aluminium shutters on his bedroom windows keeping out the daylight, and he took pills to help him get to sleep in the morning and more pills to help him rage the night away.

He tried acid but decided it was dangerous. He was gulping down uppers and downers like they were going out of fashion, but he saw himself as an anti-drug crusader. Street drugs, that is. In a bizarre incident not long before he died, Elvis made a secret journey to the White House to see the deputy director of the Narcotics Bureau. He wanted to be given a Federal Narcotics badge. It's thought he was genuine in his wish to help stamp out street drugs. But a Federal Narcotics badge would also make it okay for him to carry prescription drugs, and arms. When the deputy director refused to oblige, Elvis went to President Nixon, and a Federal Narcotics badge was formally presented to the king of rock and roll.

Who by this time was given to having target practice at hotel light bulbs and Graceland's out-buildings, and seeing angels in the waterspray.

Who in his amphetamine-ravaged mind perhaps thought — and why not indeed? — that maybe, just maybe, he was Superman. For would that be more improbable than the life he lived? And wouldn't it at least explain the awe, the sycophancy?

> People would talk and laugh until Elvis walked downstairs. As soon as he appeared everyone shut up. It was almost like turning off an electric light. There wouldn't be a sound until Elvis said something. Then people would talk softly or whisper, unless they were near Elvis. If they were close to him they just listened. Some people who were especially nervous put their cigarettes out. The pool players stopped shooting. When Elvis was in the room no one laughed at anything unless he laughed. Then everyone laughed.
>
> (Becky Yancey & Cliff Linedecker: *My Life With Elvis*)

Imagine a life where your jokes were always laughed at, where no one ever told you to stuff off or wise up or pull your head in. Where the emperor could be forever naked and no one would breath a word for they were all, in one way or another, on the payroll. What could you believe in when the truth was always fortuitously disguised?

Nik Cohn wrote:

> He had become, in fact a godhead — unseen, unreachable, more than human. The demon lover had been turned into a father, an all-powerful force that could rule his fans' lives without actually being there. His distance was a positive advantage, his artistic mistakes irrelevant, and there seemed no reason why anything should ever change. Worship, after all, is a habit that's hard to break.

During the years of keeping his distance he starred in several cretinous but phenomenally popular movies. He complained but ultimately complied. Better-quality movies were considered a financial risk and Elvis was responsible for supporting the whole Graceland caboodle in the manner to which they had all become accustomed.

And the thing about Presley's retainers is that they were, none of them, professionals. Mates became bodyguards, cousins and fans became secretaries, Daddy Vernon handled the money because he was naturally canny. Even Elvis's chubby little manager, Colonel Tom Parker, had come from the down-home tack of peepshows, carnivals, patent medicine. To read about life inside Graceland is a bit like watching the *Beverly Hillbillies*. You can't but be on their side.

And that has to be the essence of the fairy story: the reason why the hordes still make their pilgrimages to Graceland. You can stand there in your plastic sandals and know that castle belonged to an ordinary Southern boy who earned about twenty million dollars a year. And you can tell by the 'music gates', and the way the mansion glows blue and gold in the dark, that he stayed an ordinary Southern boy despite it all.

Some day I'll go to Graceland. Now that Paul Simon has made it respectable we can all go. All the same I am embarrassed by my interest; have always been embarrassed. Oh, now I can say from the safe ledge of hindsight: 'I was an Elvis fan' — but the truth is I was ambivalent. It went against the grain to

76

admire anyone unreservedly and I wanted to despise those with a natural bent for adoration.

Being a fan seemed like a non-function. I was wrong there; fans are the essential ingredient. Good biographers of rock stars talk to the fans who, on the whole, come across with a great deal more dignity and integrity than the stars. My own reluctance to align myself with the fans was nothing more than snobbery. It might have been all right to make a fool of yourself over someone obscure and intellectual like Dave Brubeck, but Elvis had two major cringe-counts going against him. One, he was popular with the masses. Two, he was working class and had neither the sense to resent it nor the grace to disguise it.

I'd like to think I'd grown past all that but even now just the thought of Elvis fans makes me cringe. I picture a gathering of stumpy males with greased sideburns and built-up heels, their spangled black shirts stretched helplessly over fat hips. Those perpetual rockers who congregate with their partners (plump and wrinkled boppers in flared skirts and Cleopatra eyeliner) in worshipful celebration. Imitation can also be the silliest form of flattery. There they are, museum pieces, the embodiment of uncool, though Elvis in his heyday was cool as could be before we even knew what the word meant.

The thing about cool is it doesn't last.

As a poor white Southern boy Elvis was brought up God-fearing. The Church of the First Assembly of God, says Becky. The magazines back in the fifties called them Holy Rollers. And for some reason we all knew, already, about the Rollers. They wrapped themselves up in white sheets and rolled ecstatically around the vestry floor — or perhaps up and down the aisles — and the amount of dirt that accumulated on the sheet in the course of all this rabid rotating was testimony to the amount of sin harboured by whoever was within the sheet. (The first religion to acknowledge the sanctity of housework?)

Clean sheets or not, the Christian churches weren't kind to Elvis in his early years of fame. Ministers of all denominations vied to be in the forefront of the righteously outraged. 'Morally insane,' pronounced one Baptist preacher, leaping into the realms of the inarguable.

Probably what got the vicars in a twist was not so much that shamelessly significant hip thrust, as an undefined — and totally justified — sense that their own power was under threat. Elvis was the harbinger of a new age.

His big contribution was that he brought it home just how economically powerful teenagers really could be. Before Elvis, rock had been a gesture of vague rebellion. Once he happened it immediately became solid, self-contained, and then it spawned its own style in clothes and language and sex, a total independence in almost everything.
(Nik Cohn: *AWopBopALooBopAWopBamBoom*)

(His other great crime was that, almost overnight, he made popular — and therefore commercial and therefore inexpungeable — what was hitherto regarded as *black* music. A commodity that white America had managed, up till then, to keep off the mainstream airwaves.)

God-fearing boys have a way of turning into God-seeking adults. During the reclusive years at Graceland, Elvis digested the momentous possibility that Adam and Eve weren't necessarily so. Whereupon he got enthused about various fringe 'spiritual' movements, the most favoured being numerology and Self Realisation. Becky blames California, where he kept hiving off to make movies. 'There's something strange about California,' she says. (Or possibly co-author Cliff Linedecker. The two of them met through a housewife from Boonville who was a mutual friend and well-known psychic.)

What with the Christians having given him the thumbs down and rock historians like Nik Cohn not yet sufficiently distanced to give him a reassuring overview of his purpose in the universe, Elvis was suffering from what-am-I-here-for? His spiritual adviser in Self Realisation was his personal hairdresser, one Larry Geller. And a couple of the leading questions Elvis hoped Larry would find the answers to (according to ex-wife Priscilla Beaulieu Presley in *Elvis and Me*) were: '. . . *why, out of all the people in the universe, he had been chosen to influence so many millions of souls. . . . And why wasn't he happy when he had more than anyone could want?*'

*   *   *

This being a fairly modern fairy-tale, the moral is largely optional. There are plenty who would say it proves that vast wealth and power should be reserved for those who have been bred to the burden of enjoying them. And, if not, the usurpers concerned should at least adapt to fit their role; should choose new and appropriate friends, acquire discretion, good taste, sophistication. (In other words, he should have learned from those who had successfully convinced themselves — or always believed — that they *deserved* to have more than anybody could possibly want.) Some people, I appreciate, find it acutely painful to think of money that could have bought a Degas being blown on dodgem cars.

But maybe the man's greatest achievement (music apart) was that he *didn't* adapt: he didn't desert his schoolmates in favour of the rich and fashionable, and his taste never improved — in fact it became marginally more execrable as the world saw in those last years when he went back to live performances dressed like the Pearly Queen.

Up till then youth had no one totally on their side except an emetic fairy called Peter Pan. Then along came Elvis Presley, who was not only staunch, but wonderfully unacceptable to most of adultdom. And, as it turned out, incorruptible in that he refused to let the world turn him into a grown-up. *Elvis Lives*, insist his disciples, regardless of ozone. Of course he does. In the soul of every constricted adolescent who dreams of escape: from anonymity, from poverty, but most of all from the grey and stifling adult fog of moderation.

But for me the real moral of the Elvis Presley story has to do with a slightly different version.

Once upon a time there was a very pretty but very lonely schoolgirl. Her father was a career officer in the Air Force and he and his family had been sent for three years to a distant land. The girl was fourteen. One of the few things she knew about that distant land before she went there was that a rich and handsome prince was also living there for a time, half disguised as a soldier and an ordinary person.

One day the schoolgirl, who missed her homeland with its

hamburgers and rock 'n' roll records, was hanging out at the American Service Club when a stranger asked her if she would like to meet the prince. The schoolgirl could hardly believe her ears. She ran home and begged her parents' permission, and, true to his word, the stranger took her to meet the prince. And of course she fell in love with him. And he asked her to come back and see him again. And again. But he was a prince and she was only fourteen.

The prince returned to his homeland but he couldn't forget the schoolgirl. He invited her to visit him at his Los Angeles house. She begged and pleaded that her parents allow her to go. And what else could her parents do — it being one thing to stop your under-age daughter from hanging about with some local lad, but quite another to prevent a prince from flying her out for a couple of weeks.

So much in love were the prince and the schoolgirl by the end of that holiday that they persuaded her parents that, once she turned sixteen, the schoolgirl should go and live in the prince's castle and attend a school nearby. For propriety's sake the arrangement was that she would be chaperoned by the prince's father and stepmother. And once again, despite their apprehensions, how could the schoolgirl's parents refuse?

As well as being handsome and rich, the prince was exceedingly generous, and having installed the schoolgirl in his palace he bought her beautiful gowns and jewels and cars and animals — anything she wanted and much that she didn't want. He taught her to dye her hair and blacken her eyes and wear her hair piled up so high she looked like a Buckingham Palace guardsman in drag. And he gave her prettily coloured pills so that even her moods could be exactly as she wanted them. (Or as *he* wanted them, which was, of course, one and the same thing.)

He was also, in his own way, very romantic and although the schoolgirl shared his bed, he insisted that she should remain technically virginal. This caused her chagrin at the time, but when in due course they got married she decided it had been really rather a nice idea.

So the schoolgirl was living a life that other schoolgirls dreamed of. And she could still scarcely believe this was happening to *her*, for her prince was desired by women throughout the kingdom and far, far beyond. Every day hundreds of adoring letters arrived for the prince and many of them were from women much more experienced than the schoolgirl. Some were even from women who were ready to ditch their husbands if they could just spend one night in the prince's bed.

But forsaking all those — at least for the meantime — the prince married the schoolgirl, thus turning her into a princess and, overnight, a woman. And nine months later they were blessed with a beautiful baby daughter.

Then, just when it was time for the Happy Ever After, the princess began to take a long hard look at the storybook world she'd stepped into and wonder why she felt so short-changed. She had beauty, wealth, respectability, maternity, and her prince, the king, was generally kind and attentive when he came home between crusades.

Yet she began to harbour strange thoughts about having a life of her own. Words like *fulfilled* and *individual* kept drifting into her beautiful head. So she went out and took lessons in dance and in martial arts and found she enjoyed these and that she had some talent. And one night when she had accompanied the king to a minor crusade at Las Vegas she told him she was leaving him.

And she packed her bags and walked right on out of the fairy story.

ten

There's nothing more depressing than a used boob tube. Contracted little monsters in lime green or fire-engine red strewn with sad old bubbles of decayed elastic. Even I, with my eternal faith in the cycles of fashion, didn't believe the human species would ever sink so low as to revive the boob tube.

Yet I couldn't bring myself to throw the wretched things away. In my musty storage room where ceiling-high stacks of clothes, all carefully sorted, lay waiting resurrection there was a litter bag full of those ridiculous garments. When I bumped against it the contents would quiver like a pile of jellyfish.

The fact of my stored boob tubes made me doubt that I was cut out to be an op-shop proprietor. I had in the past taken bets with Sha — we'd each wager millions of dollars — on the return of bell-bottoms, flared skirts and seagull collars. My philosophy was that there were only x number of things you could do with garments and everything must eventually be duplicated. Everything, that was, except the bustle and boob tubes. Still I didn't discard those little critters. In some corner of my mind I pretended that they had a future. As *fat Alice bands*, perhaps, or *thigh huggies*. No absurdity was beyond the realms of fashion.

I was convinced that the peculiarities of the used clothes business had wider philosophical application. Sometimes I'd mentally rehearse my side of an interview in which I was asked to explain the fundamental truths to be found in other people's cast-offs. Could that be the means by which I would, after all, become renowned? A philosopher of garment recycling?

It seemed a pity that the insights I'd acquired were such dismal ones. Consider this: the most-discarded garments in Auckland were the flimsy, the outrageous, the erotically inclined. While the most sought-after garments — at least in a shop like mine — were work socks, singlets and winter nightwear. Indeed, to find in the bottom of some market stall-holder's EVERYTHING 50c carton a winter nightie, or better still brushed cotton.pyjamas, was a rare and wonderful thing. So rare in fact that you could be pretty sure the previous owner had died — though not necessarily while wearing the garment in question. (I got some customers who would've liked ownership papers attached to every used bra, sweatshirt, dressing gown, in case it hadn't come from a good home. For them the thought of wearing a dead person's clothes was the worst possible scenario. I think they imagined that, in the lapse between death and rigor mortis, the corpse dragged itself to the wardrobe and tried on everything it owned in a desperate search to find something suitable for the hereafter.)

In short, the message was MOTHER WAS RIGHT. Oatmeal, wincey nighties, Milo and always rinsing twice. Such was the substance of life.

The really terrifying thing was that at forty-seven I was nearly prepared to go along with it. Already I'd got used to living alone. I could feel my own routine enclosing me easy as old slippers. I could look right through to the future — there was this nice little track running straight on, no boulders across it, no fallen trees. I'd got to thinking, what more can anyone ask?

Then Sha called in on her way south.

Hal was with her. They stayed for a couple of hours while the bus was at the garage getting its brakes relined. The others had gone off to visit friends.

I had expected a longer visit. Overnight at least. I was resentful — am I your mother or simply a pit stop? — but I kept it to myself. I wasn't prepared for the changes eight days had wrought in my little girl. Where was my unremitting iconoclast, my knocker-of-enthusiasm-in-all-its-forms? Who was this racy creature babbling gaily about tonal variations and manipulated feedback? I had an urge to reach forward and slap her sharply across the cheek like they do in the movies when someone's brain slips out of gear.

Hal didn't say much, just sat there listening to Sha with an indulgent look on his face.

And I still can't account for what happened. Perhaps I was looking at him more closely than I should have been. I just know that suddenly his eyes were looking straight into mine and I was sitting there transfixed; a lone night driver mesmerised by oncoming headlights. Bedazzled, I awaited the collision.

Then sanity and a grizzled instinct for self-preservation took over and I wrenched my eyes to the left, to the safe, stony verge of the road. Swung the wheel, teased at the brake.

Saved. But my whole body felt like a heavy metal video.

The worst of it was that I was sure he knew. Sha was telling how they arrested Willie and I sat there feeling naked and ridiculous. Ashamed of myself. I wanted to run away, to take the CLOSED sign out of the shop window and leave the two of them to their own devices. But that would have seemed a little odd and inhospitable. Sha might have wanted an explanation. Though I could see that I was, for the moment anyway, just another passing diversion in her frantically textured life.

I concentrated on the terrible tale of Willie who had discovered, when he duly appeared in the court, that he was charged not just with cannabis possession but also, inexplicably, with possessing heroin. The judge had remanded the case, insisting that Willie get himself a lawyer.

'Of course he should,' I said. I could see that Sha was properly outraged on Willie's behalf, but *heroin* is a darkly menacing word and I felt frost settling on my liberal tolerance. *No smoke without fire* it hissed and I lunged my chin towards Sha, a maternal automation: 'I bloody hope you're not...'

She stopped me with a look I probably deserved. 'See,' she said, 'it's like child molesting. People can't handle it in a rational way. Even you want to believe the worst.'

I dared, then, a fast glance that took in Hal. He had the once-removed look of someone who'd rather not become involved.

'But they must have some sort of evidence?' I persisted.

'Why must they?' Sha said. 'They produce it, who's to prove they didn't find it on him?'

'There'd have to be a reason, though.'

Hal said, 'They wanted names — suppliers. In which case

84

he'd probably have got off. But since there was no supplier. . . Catch 22.' He turned his palms up towards my stained yellow ceiling. I looked at his long fingers, his bony wrists. I thought they were beautiful.

Sha remembered that she needed clothes and rushed off to her bedroom. We could hear her crashing drawers onto the floor and swearing. The silence between us seemed almost as dangerous as my looking him in the face so I got up and busied myself at the bench, boiling up a fresh jug and doing useful things with water crackers.

And I made myself think about young Willie, caught like a white mouse in a maze that had no purpose. Not innocent though, as Sha implied. He'd had a bit of herb in his pocket — left himself wide open to at least the crime of stupidity.

That made me sorry for myself: Ms average taxpayer who had for years been contributing to helicopters, police salaries, prisons, probation officers and so on, all to what end? I could get quite worked up just thinking of how many pointless projects, schemes, laws I'd involuntarily contributed towards in my working life, and how many times my views, as a taxpayer, have been libellously invented. . . distorted. . . misrepresented. Never once consulted — unless you grab at straws and count an election as consultation.

I was slashing butter onto the crackers and waiting for Hal to attempt some kind of conversation, if only for convention's sake. My silence wasn't gamesmanship, just a lack of something suitable to say and the fear that once my mouth opened under the circumstances I would babble.

I sliced cheese and placed it on the crackers. Sha was still crashing about in her bedroom talking to herself, or maybe singing — it was hard to tell. Hal was sitting at the table in the corner of my eye.

I sliced gherkins and put them on the cheese on the crackers. The silence leaned in on me until I could hardly breathe. 'It looks like,' I said quickly, 'I'm gonna have to move.'

'How come?' Conversational. No undertones, no overtones. I set the crackers between us and told him about the man called Hargreaves. I pulled myself together and turned him back into an ordinary beat-up looking guy wolfing crackers at my kitchen table. I could look at his hands with no urge to zoom in and linger in close-up.

Hormonal, I thought. The first attack of menopause, which I'd known was waiting for me, like a rapist round some dark corner. But, as with rape, I'd had this secret vanity that it wouldn't happen to me: I was much too sussed to suffer such an *obvious* disaster.

Hal gave me the same advice as Tom, Miriam's schoolteacher husband. 'Make them buy you out,' he said. 'Decide an amount and triple it. They want you out, they'll pay.' He saw my expression. 'That's how they operate, Kath.' It was the first time he'd used my name instead of that silly ironic 'Mother'.

'Maybe,' I said, 'it's not how *I* operate.'

'Ha.' He thought that was funny. Or just absurd? 'Well naturally,' he said, '*they* haven't quite reached the spiritual and philosophical heights of . . .' he jerked his head in the direction of my shop.

'Ha,' I said. It was my turn. 'Ha ha.'

Hal lurched forward and looked into my eyes. A tiny piece of cracker was caught in the corner of his mouth. 'Believe me,' he said, 'they'll respect you for it.'

Then I laughed. It was a mistake because I got caught up in his eyes again. They trapped me, like a web. I had to get up and blunder off to see what Sha was doing.

She was stapling an old fox fur — the kind with the head attached — to her denim jacket. 'Come back in there,' I told her, 'he's your friend.'

'Is he?' she said, and she gave me — I thought — a long look. But she came, anyway. By then his eyes and my laugh and the words that brought it about seemed to have happened a long time before.

> She came from Port Arthur, Texas, and looked like a big tough woman. On stage she drank straight from the bottle and stomped, did the grind. She cussed a lot and her voice was raucous, full of strength and guts. Sometimes she sounded brutal and commanding, sometimes hurt, and she would pick her songs up to annihilate them, leave them crippled ever after.
>
> (Nik Cohn again, in *AWopBopALooBopAWopBamBoom*)

86

After Sha and Hal had gone I left the CLOSED sign on the window though it was only halfway through the afternoon. I put *Cheap Thrills* on the turntable and opened the bottle of Jack Daniels that I'd bought for Clive's birthday. He would be forty-eight.

I dragged the wooden settee over next to the doorway so that, with the door propped open, I could see right through the Second Gear window to the street.

By five-thirty, four possible customers had stomped about irritably, peering in. But I was drunk by then and remorseless. I flipped the record once again and turned the volume up to frenzy level. On my behalf Janis Joplin plucked out her heart, assaulted angels, pulverised the world.

eleven

They were driving down the Kapiti coast, passing through towns as familiar and indistinguishable as any corner dairy. Hal, staring vacantly at the squat little shops pressed together like roosting hens, remembered how, looking out at other towns in other countries, he would feel a wrench of longing for these towns that were like small towns everywhere, but at the same time different.

Homesickness had been those intermittent and unsourced visions of such towns, just as he saw them right now: night-lit, deserted and moving on a fast screen. For a few seconds he would feel sick with yearning for stupid little burgs that no one in his right mind would dream of living in.

In the light of Levin his own reflection looked back at him, gaunt. He remembered a perfect moment at least eighteen years before of seeing his face beside him, disembodied but entirely satisfactory. He was travelling by train to Wellington after a week of studio work in Auckland, and in three days he and the rest of Belinda's Nightmare would be in Sydney. He'd looked at himself, ghostly in the train window, and seen for certain his own difference; that he looked like an artist or a musician. That is, he looked *interesting*. A face that would produce well: that's what he'd thought. Meaning publicity not progeny. He'd ordered his memory to treasure that moment.

Beyond the town the night was thick as mist. Hal could smell the sea, but only with his eyes closed.

When he opened them again there was a solitary house lit up and uncurtained. A man and a woman sat at a table. He wore a bathrobe, she was wearing a green nightgown. Between them was a bottle. They weren't young, and her uncombed mess of hair suggested they were well and truly married. Yet they were leaning towards each other eagerly, like lovers.

Hal pressed against the window watching until they were out of sight. The man and woman gave him the same melancholy twang he used to get thinking about those small towns. Yet domesticity appalled him. The pleasure of seeing it through lighted windows had always been that he was the one moving on in the dark.

Behind him Sha and the sulky young woman Kevin had picked up in Napier were whispering together. Kevin was up front with George, who drove in steady silence. Across from the girls Cosmo, eyes closed, was plugged to his Walkman. At the back Willie sat hunched up in psychic pain. There weren't many spare seats. The back half of the bus was walled off, contained their gear. It was an old Road Services bus, built to carry mail and newspapers, plus a few seats up front for passengers prepared to travel in the early hours of the morning. Hal turned back to the window. In Levin a public clock had showed 01.45.

The motel had fucked up and booked them for two nights instead of three. Which turned out to be a real problem because that weekend was a big one on the Palmerston North social calendar: National Girl Guides' Convention, drag racing and the Pan Pacific marching finals. They decided in the end to drive straight through to Wellington after the gig.

Hal knew they considered him responsible for this dreary ride. He'd set the tour up and decided against a manager. Managers were never a guarantee of smooth running, but they needed someone to blame. (And, privately, Hal had been glad to get out of that city where his past fumbled and whined for attention.)

All along Hal had seen this as his last tour. He'd thought of promoting it that way but it seemed to imply people would care, and perhaps no one would. Certainly the pleasure of being on the road, this time, seemed muted. The couple in the window had not struck him as pitiable, and that was a worry. His old certainties were shifting beneath him.

He wanted Sha curled up in the seat beside him. He tried her out in a nightdress and wayward hair sitting across the table from him on a sleepless dawn and it was dangerously appealing.

He'd always had a policy of not being the partner with most to lose.

He disliked the way Sha had chummed up with Kevin's bimbo, as if there was no distinction to be made between the two of them. He wanted her in the seat beside him, her stupid spindly hair brushing his cheek. He wanted her there, still and sleepy with her smart mouth temporarily at rest.

Hal liked his women young. Who didn't? And Sha was no younger than some who had been before, yet this time he was more conscious of the gap. She made him feel insecure, even deferential. Somehow, in his mind, she'd come to represent THE AUDIENCE. Mysterious, judgmental, intolerant, inconsistent, but most of all, *young*. Despite himself, he sought her opinions and feared them. Her existence edged him closer to obsolescence. Yet he seemed to need her. *Eighteen years apart*, he thought and the humiliation was intense.

> *You undermine me,*
> *You un-define me,*
> *I'm the past perfect and you're the future tense*

Another house lit up. Curtained. Cars outside. Party inside.
'Whoa over,' Kevin was saying to George. 'We could crash it. They'd be rapt on account of us being slightly famous.'

> *Put us together and we don't make sense.*

'You're just no fun at all,' said Kevin in a camp voice.
'I'm not in a party mode,' George told him.

> *I'm in a you mode,*
> *Are you in a me mode?*
> *We could get together and work out a new code*
> *For living.*

It was five years at least since Hal tired of modest failures and stopped writing his own material. His lyrics had begun to sound antediluvian — positively Noël Coward. Even now if he tried these out on Sha she would snigger.

In the late sixties Hal and the Belinda's bass player, Pete Pengelly, used to collaborate. Peter came up with lyrics that were wonderfully obscure. Years later, when they met up in New

York, Pete had confessed to Hal that he stole them straight from the *Reader's Digest*. He would clip a paragraph or two into clumps of words, scatter them on the floor then arrange them in the order he retrieved them. The *Sydney Sun* reviewer wrote of 'Dylanesque depths which lend an intellectual substance lacking in their first album'. Something like that. Hal had long since lost the clipping and the album.

If this was Hal's last tour, what then? All he knew was music and getting by. And possibly Sha. Whereas Willie had his Spiritual Search, and Kevin had his Racial Pride and George had Annie and the boys and a home with paddocks. And Cosmo . . . Cosmo had his Stevie Ray Vaughan hat.

Peeking like a sniper over the back of the seat Hal saw that Kevin's girl had fallen asleep on Sha who was freeing herself with the edgy concentration of a knitter untangling wool. Hal let his head fall against the seat, pretending sleep so he could pretend to be awoken. His body glinted with anticipation, like small waves in morning sunlight. He brushed a hand over his mouth and sure enough the corners had curled up, so he forced them down with a finger and thumb.

The man at the bank did that the once when Hal asked for a serious loan. The gesture was supposed to imply judicious consideration. He wasn't the manager of the bank. Even wearing his one pair of Joe 90 trousers Hal didn't rate a manager. Monetarists can't cope with people who may have found something they enjoy more than spending money.

Sha didn't join Hal. He was forced to peek again. She was with Willie in the back. She was twisting a Bounty Bar packet between her hands. The packet split and she shook out the two little chocolate bars. She put one in Willie's mouth. It was not quite an intimate gesture; she had the slightly exasperated air of a mother bird feeding its young. Hal imagined the taste of chocolate-coated coconut and hoped Willie got what was coming to him.

He — Willie, that is — had made another appearance at the Kaikohe District Court, to everyone's considerable inconvenience. He had applied for legal aid and been appointed a local solicitor, to whom Willie had made a couple of toll calls making it clear he did not intend to plead guilty. The lawyer was unable to see Willie before the court opened, but in a hasty conversation during the lunch recess (Willie still hadn't been called) he explained that he'd been unable to locate a police officer who was able or prepared to discuss the case. Therefore he didn't know whether the prosecution intended to proceed or if they were open to a 'deal'. He recommended that they should ask for another remand, during which he would 'sound out' the police.

'But,' said Willie, 'you've had three weeks. And anyway, why should I do a deal? I told you, I had a bit of dope in my pocket, in an old mustard tin. Wouldn'ta even filled half a matchbox. And they took that, and I'm not denying it, but that was all. So that's what you tell them and let's just get it done with, *please.*'

'It doesn't work like that,' said the lawyer. 'Besides, they might have found the hard stuff in your motel room — that's the sort of thing I need to find out.'

(He looked to be in his thirties, the lawyer, and he fancied himself as streetwise. That is, he didn't talk about 'pot', and he countered Willie's fears by saying, 'You and Keith Richards. That can't be so bad.')

'They didn't,' said Willie. 'How could they?'

'That's the point,' said the lawyer. 'You can't be sure.'

'I'm sure,' said Willie.

Yet when he rejoined the band and repeated the whole conversation he stared at the other four in a wild, pleading way as if to say, 'Was it? . . . admit it . . . say it was yours and save me.'

In fact, before the lawyer had a chance to say anything the prosecution asked for a remand, saying they were still waiting for the results of analysis. Willie wanted it over and done with, before some nosy reporter discovered who he was and told the world and Willie's father Duncan Crowley.

When Willie — he was fifteen, still at school — joined his first band (Ms Marples, a three-piece with a singer who resembled Boy George), they got a lot of unsolicited, but not entirely unwelcome publicity. Reporters fell over each other trying to suggest there was something ironic/wasteful/heart-warming/ominous about the boy's after-school activities. The attention surged again when he left school (and home) a year later to play professionally with Mordant What. But it was something less than scandal and they soon lost interest.

Although he'd lived for sixteen years in Duncan Crowley's opulent mansion on the Takapuna foreshore Willie had seen little of his father, who had other houses and younger and more prepossessing children. As far back as he could remember, encounters with Duncan Crowley had brought Willie out in ugly, itching spots.

Having been remanded, Willie waited in the foyer for the lawyer, who had other cases to attend to. When eventually he appeared Willie suggested Hal or George could be a character witness. The lawyer snorted and said, given their occupation, that would probably do more harm than good. Willie took this to mean the lawyer thought that Willie must use heroin because he was a musician.

'So get another lawyer then,' said George.

'What with?' Willie's eyes were red with held-back tears.

No one else could take that problem seriously. Duncan Crowley was a multimillionaire.

'Tell your father.'

'No no no no no.' He blinked around at them pitifully. 'Why are they doing this to me?'

No one was certain. 'Because you pissed them off,' said Kevin. 'Shit, they do worse for less if it's one of us.'

Hal didn't feel responsible for Willie's anguish. If Willie wouldn't go to his father for help at least he should tell his lawyer — who would tell the police — who that father *is*.

What if Hal came clean and gave evidence? No, he couldn't. Confessions needed to be early or not at all. Besides the solution was in Willie's hands. And life had already given Willie so much advantage. Not just wealth, but talent.

When Willie played well he made magic. Brutal and ecstatic or sweet and insidious, his music came out like mountains weeping; that vast and inconceivable. So he had a face like an uncooked pie, but who could tell — that might be the right face for the 1990s. Just as Hal's face had been perfect for the seventies. And passable for the eighties.

But Hal had sensed early, with no real regret, that he was never going to be up there scrambling among the superstars.

He was a cruiser, good enough to get by. He had resilience but no fire. And he was too busy looking back and being pleasantly surprised by how far he'd got to care sufficiently about how much further others might go.

The sky was getting light as they came into Wellington. George was doing 100 ks on an empty motorway.

'Imagine being recognised?' said Kevin. 'Imagine if a friend drove past and saw us. We practising driving for the handicapped or something?'

George smiled.

The harbour opened out to them, sparkling grey. When Hal was a child the shingle in their driveway glittered like diamonds. It was pale and brilliant and in the rain it smelt sulphuric, like the burnt heads of matches. But when his father left no one ever renewed the shingle. After a while there was only the odd sparkle at the edge of the grass to remind Hal of how it had been.

Sha stood for a few seconds peering out the windows at the harbour, then she flopped into the seat next to Hal. She smiled at him, an edgy fired-up smile. The girl who'd been allowed to join the circus.

'You hungry?' he mumbled hopefully. She shook her head, staring out past him at the city taking shape against the water.

'I am,' he said.

'Boo boo, der der, neh mind.' She patted his cheek.

George braked, smooth but sudden — the bus stopped in the left-hand lane.

'George,' yelled Kevin, 'for fucksake.'

Kevin's girl woke up, complaining.

'Where are we going?' said George. 'That's what I want to know. Which lane?'

'Where d'you want to go?' asked Hal, of everyone. And they answered . . . pie cart . . . bed . . . home . . . Los Angeles.

'George,' said Kevin, 'we constitute a hazard. Just bloody move will you.'

Sha had laid her hand on Hal's shoulder and her fingers suddenly bit into his flesh. Looking at her face he saw that happiness had caught her off guard.

twelve

It's an old expression,' said Cosmo. 'American. You went to an
A & P show or something and you didn't win anything at the
sideshows, they'd say *at least you got to hear the band play.* So
this guy who wrote a book about the Stones and Altamont and all
that, well he says that was the scene.'

'Stanley Booth,' said Hal.

'Hey?'

'Guy that wrote the book.'

'Prob'ly, was some nerdy sort of name. You read it then?'

'Nah. Jus' like to drop names.'

'Ha.'

'Whaddya mean *that was the scene*?' Kevin. 'I don't want to be
unkind, Cos, but you talk some fearful crap sometimes.'

'Least I have opinions. *Of my own.* What I meant was all the
hangers-on-ers and that, just wanting to feel they were part of it.
Well, that's what everyone wants, isn't it? Least once in a lifetime.
They wanna get to hear the band play.'

'So you're lucky,' said Kevin.

'*This*? I don't mean this. I don't mean here, man. I mean out
there where it's really happening.'

'It's the same everywhere,' said Hal. 'A bit sharper, a bit faster,
but the same.'

'I'm talking Big Time. Fame. Megabucks. Suites at the Hyatt.'

'Who?'

'Whaddya mean?'

'Who you talking about?'

'Christ, anyone — I dunno.'

'Michael Jackson?'

'Phwwhh.'

'Stones?'

'Don't make me laugh. They're used, man. They're last year's newspaper.'

'Pogues then? Tracy Chapman?'

'I'm not talking music, I'm talking ... I dunno, *scene.*'

'Guns 'n' Roses, U2.'

'Yeah — but no ... guess I just missed out. It's all got kind of boring now.'

'I'm not bored,' said Kevin. 'Unless we're talking about this precise moment in time, listening to you.'

George came in and stood by the door.

'It's different for you,' said Cosmo. 'I'm a professional hanger-on. All I ever wanted was to get to hear the band play but seems like I'm too late. They've packed up and gone.'

'To heaven, mostly.'

'Maybe they've come back already,' said Hal. 'As parakeets. Or snails.'

'Not Marley,' said Kevin. 'Never a snail. No.'

'A hedgehog,' said Cosmo. 'The Bogor kind. With dreads.'

'Cosmo wants the seventies back,' Hal told George.

George said, 'Willie's been on the phone to his lawyer again. They've changed the date. It's now the seventeenth. We're playing in Christchurch that night.'

'They'll have to change it. He'll have to say he won't be available.'

'He thinks that's what they want.' George stretched open his eyes. 'He thinks they checked out our dates and changed it deliberately.'

Cosmo and Kevin grinned. Hal shook his head.

'So why doesn't he come in and tell us himself?' said Cosmo.

'He thinks we've all got hostile.'

'He's bloody right,' said Kevin. 'I mean, Jesus Christ!'

No one said, 'It's one of those things.' Or, 'There but for the grace of God.'

'He'll have to change it and that's it,' said Hal.

'He reckons,' said George, 'the longer it drags on the more chance some local reporter'll cotton on to who he is. He thinks if it was heard in the morning he could maybe get back in time.'

'From Kaikohe? Tell him get real.'

'I've done my telling,' said George and helped himself to a can of beer. 'A lot of it's myth,' he said to Cosmo. 'The seventies. Those who thought they were having the best time were the ones who were losing their brain cells fastest. It was mostly hype and orange velvet.'

'Still,' said Cosmo. 'Look at the music.'

'True,' said George. 'Santana. Saw them in concert year after I left school. It was like being in the sun for the first time. Never held a stick in my life but I saw that Mike Shrieve, he was just a kid then, and I thought, I'm gonna do that.'

'That's it. Same with me really. My Dad took me to the first Stones tour. Me and my sister. I's only a real little kid. And I saw these guys come on, fucking about, blowing in the mikes, dragging these bloody great extension cords. And I thought, hey. An' I thought, Cosmo baby, *that is you.*'

'I went to see Cliff Richard,' said Kevin, 'and the minute he kinda bounced onto —'

Cosmo threw an empty can. It hit Kevin on the chest. He clutched it to him and hurled himself against the unmade bed.

'And he scores again.' Kevin's voice was muffled by duvet. 'This man is invincible.'

'Born out of my time,' lamented Cosmo. 'Body paint... embroidered incense holders... I could've really got into all that.'

George said, 'I was with this outfit called The Mildred Experience. We had a frenzied lute player, that was our thing. Humour and psychedelia, you see. We were living up the Hokianga. Four families on the land, all that. Other people like us all around and everyone was into, you know, doing their own thing. So we got together, got our gear and all and we used to practise in an old woolshed 'cos everyone was into letting the land revert and all that. Well, practice night they'd all turn up. First few times we thought great, we've got all this community support and everything. But it wasn't that at all. They'd all come to perform.

'There were these closet singers who thought they were Patti Smith or Lou Reed. "I don't exactly sing," they'd say, "it's more kind of *delivering.*" And there were these straight poets who'd get up and order that we provide some arty little accompaniment in the background. And there was the odd acid-inspired exhibitionist who wanted to strip to something graunchy. So we'd have maybe six songs we'd planned to go over but never did because people were hogging the mike and dragging out tambourines and, you know, *being creative.*

'Some nights we just gave up and packed up our gear and left. Long as we left them the microphone and the amps and stuff they wouldn't even notice.

'You'd see them next day and they'd say, "Hey, really dug you guys last night. Bloody fantastic. When's your next practice night?" '

thirteen

He rang — John Hargreaves, the company man — to see if I'd come up with anything. I said, 'Listen chum, I've got customers to serve, stock to buy — and wash and iron — accounts to keep, GST returns to fill in. I don't sit in an air-conditioned office dreaming up new ways of fiddling my executive expense account.'

I wanted to say.

In fact, I said I was still looking. I lied, but in a firm tone of voice. After that I rang around some real estate places and found a couple that deigned to bother with business tenants. Then I rang Miriam's and got Tom who said she was at a seminar in Christchurch. I said she might run into Sha since they were heading down that way. When I hung up I wondered if in fact Miriam hadn't been there beside the phone gesturing at Tom, not wanting to speak to me. I'd started having thoughts like that, living alone.

I rang my friend Rose, who was there, and understood and could spare Friday. Rose worked on contract for a PR firm. They paid her by the hour. The rate was good but she didn't get many hours of work a week. I suspect she was too efficient. She feared she was not efficient enough — *effective* enough she called it — and waited for the day her head would roll onto the hushed pink carpet.

As an examiner of premises she was overly effective. That Friday, on my behalf, she would open cupboards and run water taps in buildings so remote from civilisation the only beings to set foot in them would be schoolboys with compasses built into the heels of their shoes. We would clatter across miles of tarmac, around and between panelbeaters, upholsterers, office suppliers, and up an outside staircase — lethally slippery — then edge our way into some windowless cell the agent would unsmilingly describe as a showroom. And Rose would begin to examine door hinges and light fixtures as if we were property moguls and the place had possibilities.

In the late afternoon, and by then visibly losing patience, the agent took us to a place in Kingsland. A nice little low-slung shop with peeling paint and decent windows. My heart raised its head for the first time all day — and instinct was my only arbiter. There was another op shop not even a block away, but that wasn't necessarily a bad thing; together we might draw people from other suburbs. Op shopping was a kind of an urban picnic; people liked to make a day of it.

So the agent led us into the showroom and I didn't mind at all when Rose shoulder-tackled the counter to see if it was built-in. I could see at once where I would put the racks, and just out the back there was a storage room with masses of shelving. I gave Rose a nod.

The living quarters were up a flight of unpainted and uncarpeted wooden stairs. Aesthetically fine, but noisy. The flat itself was better than fine. It had a skylight. It was like an artist's studio. And because it was so light and without curtains or blinds — and so empty — it seemed large. I forgot Rose's instructions and smiled at the agent.

'Most likely kauri,' he was saying. 'Absolutely solid. If you like these old places, this one's a gem.'

He stood for a moment at a side window looking down at the street. I stepped forward to take a look for myself — and my foot went through the floor. I slid down like a ballet dancer with my right leg thrust forward until it was horizontal. The other leg went straight down. I could feel blood forming sluggish little rivers on my scraped thigh. And below that I could feel the broken, biscuity edges of the ceiling.

I moved the absent leg very tentatively. The ceiling was about knee level and I seemed to have broken off rather a lot of it. My respectable-tenant skirt was spread out all around me. I noticed the glint of a safety pin where the hem had come unstitched.

The agent was still at the window staring at me as if I was something unscheduled and unfortunate — maybe a dog turd. I craned around till I could see Rose standing at the entrance to the kitchen alcove. I gave her a desperate look. I was dismayed that it seemed necessary, but she was just standing there looking first at me and then at the agent. When I eased my neck back towards him he was still in the same place. Frowning, it seemed, but the light was behind him; I couldn't be sure. I began to wonder if I ought to scream.

I pushed my hands down against the floor and tried to ease myself up but the boards on either side of my thigh had a vice grip. I have the kind of thighs that touch each other; they plump out then narrow again at the groin. What went in would not necessarily come out.

When I looked behind again Rose was edging her way towards me like a soldier crossing a minefield. About two metres away she stopped and held out her hand. I reached round and my hidden leg shrieked in pain. I grasped Rose's hand and she pulled. But I'm fatter than Rose — her thighs only wave to each other — and nothing moved.

We both looked at the agent. He appeared to be catatonic. Rose came cautiously closer. We examined the boards on either side of my leg. They seemed to be solid.

'I guess we'll have to pull one up,' said Rose, looking at the agent.

The agent moved a little closer but said nothing.

Rose tried to move the board.

'We'll need some kind of lever.'

She looked again at the agent, wanting some sort of authorisation. I would have done the same but I was angry at her. Denied permission would she just leave me there like some art nouveau light fitting?

A new pain reminded me that my subterranean foot was *flexed* (as they say in aerobic classes) to the point of rigidity. Quite on its own initiative it was clutching at the shred of dignity afforded by my old black shoe, dangling it from my toes. I carefully disengaged my ankle and could just hear the shoe land on the showroom floor far, far below.

In a kitchen cupboard Rose eventually found a balding hearthbrush. While she was searching, the agent wouldn't meet my eye.

Intrepid now about crossing the floor, she managed to wedge

the hearthbrush between the board and a four-by-two beneath. We watched the nails being pried loose. At that point the agent leant forward and gripped the board and together they pulled it up. 'Don't look down,' he advised me, but I did. I saw the broken ceiling — almost certainly asbestos — and, way beneath, a black slip-on shoe among the debris.

Rose was semi-hysterical all the way home. I could get no sense out of her. 'Should I take it?' I wanted to know, but even that would send her into another bout of terrible mirth.

That night as I was re-examining my abrasions, she rang. 'It just dawned on me,' she said. 'He was petrified.'

'What?'

'That bloke. He thought you were going to sue.'

'It wasn't *his* fault.'

'All the same.'

'Maybe I should.' I pressed a finger against my thigh to gauge the price of my pain. A couple of hundred dollars?

'You can't,' she said. 'Because of accident compensation.'

'Oh.'

'Just thought you'd like to know.'

'But. . .' I said.

'Right. Bye.'

As she was hanging up she must have had a flashback. I could hear her giggles breaking loose like pebbles from a sodden cliff face. I decided to give the place a miss.

Three days later John Hargreaves called. Smiling. He thought he had the perfect premises. He was so pleased with himself, I didn't even ask where. We made a date for after work.

He picked me up in a seamless, noiseless car. We turned into Shelly Beach Road. 'Where is it?' I asked.

'Glenfield.'

My heart slumped and sulked, round-shouldered. 'I can't live on the Shore.'

He gave me the very same long-suffering smile I used to give to Sha in her nihilistic phase. It threw me quite badly. I knew so well how it felt to be the smiler — that combination of wise, infuriated and a bit of a phoney. I didn't know how to be the recipient of such a smile. I looked out the side window. I *can't*

102

live on the Shore. I *won't* live on the Shore.

'All this prejudice,' he said. 'From both sides. It's rather childish.'

I sighed. Heavily, so it wouldn't be wasted. 'In my business,' I said slowly, as if I was presenting some complex philosophical argument, 'the right area is all-important.'

'Exactly. And Glenfield is largely a working-class area. This idea that the North Shore is full of yuppies is just a myth.' The car was like a rental, so tidy and impersonal. Did he have a family? Children who played hockey on Saturday mornings? A dog?

I called Rose in my head. *Hi*. 'Where are you?' *Glenfield*. 'GLENFIELD?!!!'

Might as well be Outer Mongolia. No one would come and visit me. 'Shit, Kath, I'd never find it — always get lost on the Shore. And you know how they drive over there.'

For the first time it hit me that Second Gear would become a pile of rubble. That I would lose those largely nameless friends who were its customers. Who came to fill in time, to browse through my 50c and $1 boxes, to treat themselves to the extravagance of a $3 dress. Or, after school, to clothe sulking kids who would try to hide behind the racks, afraid they would be *seen* inside my shop. Even worse, be seen inside the clothes that came from my shop. And I realised I loved those women; loved our shapeless conversations about the government, the weather, kidsthesedays and the prices you had to pay in real shops.

Would they miss me?

'Where do you live?' I asked John Hargreaves.

'Browns Bay.' The Shore, of course. He didn't even smile.

Three suburbs later he said, 'It's a growth area, the Shore, however you look at it. People still have jobs, money in their pockets. And in any business — I don't care what it is — that's the most important thing. People having money in their pockets.'

Not in mine, I wanted to say. Not in my business, boyo. But on the Shore you lose the courage to be heretical.

'Well, here we are,' he said flicking on his left blinker. We weren't in a shopping centre, nothing. Just this busy highway lined with non-committal brick houses. Then, on a corner, up against the footpath, a sagging dairy with its tiny window stuck about with torn and fly-spotted posters for ice-cream and cigarettes. We parked right outside.

Rage paralysed me.

'Don't worry about locking the door,' he said, 'it's automatic.'

I got out of the car and followed him across the footpath. The bubble-glass panels on the door were obscured by faded ice-blocks. He unlocked the door and we went in. It was suicide territory; small, dark and fetid. We went through to the living quarters behind. I was too outraged to pass comment.

The living room was semi-furnished. We had to squeeze past a greasy orange sofa. The kitchen was separate. I looked from the door at the encrusted taps, the jars, the litter bag, the two dead pot plants.

'We could get it cleaned up a bit,' he said, a tad defensive.

'Wait till you see the apple tree,' he said, shouldering open the misshapen back door.

He beckoned me, but I didn't step out. I didn't need to. The apple tree *was* the back yard. It covered it like an umbrella.

'Great shade,' said John Hargreaves. 'Pity the sun's not out.'

I looked for the sky and saw three wizened yellow apples. A few more had fallen to the ground and lay rotting beside the dog kennel and rusted motor mower engine and the pile of stubby green bottles. *Rotten peaches*, I thought in an Elton John whine.

I didn't want to travel back to the city with someone who had so severely insulted me. But a taxi would cost a fortune and I'd never find a public phone, let alone a bus. By the time we reached the bridge I'd grown ashamed of my silence. Look at it his way. A businessman. To him there's new and old; upmarket and downmarket. Who would expect him to understand the distinctions between down-at-heel and disgusting?

Nevertheless there was a warning to be taken. I had just been shown his company's estimate of my worth. I should find a lawyer right away. A cheap lawyer. Who would appreciate the simple dignity of my trade. Ha ha.

I asked to be dropped at K Road. It was late-night shopping and the bargain tables were spread along the crowded pavements. I needed to hang out there a while, to be surrounded by the casual comfort of strangers. Regular people, the kind who could get a kick out of a $5 discount.

He said as I closed the door, 'There is some urgency.'

'Yes,' I said. 'I know. I'll be in touch.'

The lock button on the passenger side clicked down before he drove off.

There was something I needed to buy, but I could only remember the sense of needing to remember what it was. I poked about at a few of the stalls, feeling an urge to spend money, make a transaction, treat myself. *I shop therefore I am*, as the slogan artist said. There was an extraordinary array of merchandise I neither needed nor wanted. For a moment I wished John Hargreaves was with me to witness. Money in my pocket, but staying there.

Eventually I wandered into the second-hand record shop. Looking through the As. Armatrading (I had already), Amazing Rhythm Aces (they didn't have). . . I glanced down at the Bs, the stack left ajar by the person before me, and there was that long jaw, those gently Neanderthal features. HAL BARBER. The cover photo was black and white and years ago. His face loomed from a black background. His hair was shoulder-length, a central part brushed back like stage curtains. All seventies and soulful.

I touched it tentatively, but the shock had been on first sight. Then it had snatched me up and hurled me across the room, above the imported selection and the young couple fighting in undertones beside Heavy Metal. Now there was just the fluidly enfeebled sensation of convalescence.

Good $6 said the handwritten sticker on the right-hand side. I knew 'good' referred to the record's condition but I preferred to see it as an affirmation of life and coincidence. I would've bought the thing even if every track was gouged to hell, just for the picture on the cover.

'Haven't seen you for a while,' said the owner as he manoeuvred Hal into a paper bag.

'Too busy,' I said. The truth was I'd usually come in either with Sha or on her behalf. Buying records just for myself had seemed an extravagance.

'So how's things?'

I shrugged. 'You know.'

He smiled at me. We didn't know each other well but we knew that we were similar kind of people. I'm never sure if that has to do with appearances, or is just an instinct. I had this rather illogical conviction that there weren't many people like him and me on the North Shore.

As I was about to go I had a sudden flash of the record that had been behind Hal's in the stack. I'd seen it yet not seen it. And I remembered what it was I'd been meaning to shop for — a present for Clive.

His birthday gathering had been one of life's more depressing occasions. For a start, I had forgotten it. It was only when he rang harassed, to ask me to bring some glasses, that my memory came stumbling back.

'Glasses?' I wasn't even dressed.

'I was afraid you'd have left. And maybe plates. Little plates, you know. What d'you think they'll expect? I've got some French bread. And tomatoes, and fancy cheese and some ginger-and-walnut paté. I don't know what it's like. Have you tried it? D'you think that sounds enough? And I made this dip to have with corn chips, but it smells pretty weird.'

'Whaddis it taste like?'

'Dunno. I'm not game to try. So? You think it's enough?'

'How many people?'

'About twenty, I think. That I've asked. But some of them probably won't come. But on the other hand they might, and they might bring friends.'

'Don't worry. Sounds fine. And I'll pick up something from the bakery. Plates and glasses. Anything else?'

'What about peanuts. Should I get some peanuts?'

'You want peanuts?'

'Not me. But other people might, d'you think?'

'I'll bring some peanuts. Stop worrying. And they'll bring stuff — it's your birthday.' I remembered the Jack Daniels, Clive's birthday present, was two-thirds empty. And no other booze in the place, not even a bottle of cheap wine. It was Sunday.

All told there were nine people, including me and Clive. I took it as a warning; this is what happens when you're forty-eight and *partnerless*. Two of them I knew. They were old friends of Clive. Then there was a smarmy-looking young guy who worked for Parks and Reserves, a couple who had just left their respective spouses and children in order to be with each other, a woman who taught science at the school Clive was employed by, and her husband — a bloated academic with sceptical lips.

Despite the peanuts and the French bread and the five kinds of cheese, despite the six-packs and the casks and a couple of bottles of Aussie champagne and my third of a bottle of Jack Daniels, as a party it had about as much life as wet kindling. By the time I arrived Clive had stopped worrying about his hostly obligations and was getting rapidly and depressively drunk. He hugged me in the kitchen as I unpacked the plates, the glasses and an Edna Everage gateau, covered in glacé cherries, angelica, edible ball-bearings, chocolate shavings and jellybeans. I thought for a minute he'd collapsed against my neck, the embrace was so limp and prolonged.

'It was the only cake they had left,' I apologised.

He detached himself and studied the thing. 'No licorice all-sorts,' he whined.

'Tough,' I said.

Clive smiled. *Bravely*. It was really that kind of smile. I wanted to bang his head about I felt so angry. *You've got us here, kiddo. We came. So shape up. Don't do this to your friends.*

'No candles either,' I said, ignoring the smile.

'Don't need them,' he said. 'Sandi made me one with candles.' He opened a cupboard and there was a real birthday cake with icing like a stormy ocean, and candles.

'Twenty-six,' he said to save me counting.

'Twenty-six?'

'She let me choose. I thought it was probably my best year, being twenty-six.'

'Why? What happened?'

'Nothing in particular. Not that I can remember.'

I pulled out the peanuts and the whiskey bottle. 'Clive, I did a terrible thing. I had this present for you, then in a moment of . . . emotional crisis . . . I drank it. But I'm going to get you something else. Promise.'

'Don't worry,' he said. 'Nobody else has.'

He saw the look on my face — not sure whether I should kiss him better or kick him to death — and suddenly laughed. I poured myself a nip of bourbon. 'Shall we mingle?' 'If you think it's absolutely necessary.' 'Someone has to do something.' *Do you live round here? How do you know Clive? Yes, a very kind man, that's the kind of thing he would do. Do you have a job? Right. No such thing as job security, not any more, not these days. Did you know there's blood on the back of your skirt?*

The schoolteacher proved to be a waver. Whenever a joint was handed round she sucked at it like a vacuum cleaner, but when Sandi and her husband John lit regular cigarettes the schoolteacher turned into a human windscreen wiper. John slunk outside looking like a pre-schooler who'd just fouled himself but Sandi caught my eye, winked and stood her ground. She gave the schoolteacher the kind of uneasily sympathetic look that spastic people arouse and continued to send out smoke.

I was feeling so unrelaxed I even made small talk with Clive. *So howzthingzanyway?* 'Have I seen you since my uncle died?' *Is this a trick question or something?* 'I'm serious. He died. He left me his holiday house. Wattle Bay. Know where that is?' *West. Right across the harbour.* 'No one else's heard of it.' *So. You gonna move there?* 'You wanta see it?' *You don't want to live there?* 'We could go down next weekend.' *Sometime anyway.* 'You'll like it. I know you'll like it.' *What about Canada? Thought you were going back?* 'Nah.' *So are you gonna rent it, or what?* 'Depends, I dunno.' *Depends?* 'Right. You gonna come and see it?'

About then the Parks and Reserves lad beckoned Clive away and started whispering urgently. Clive looked across at the middle-aged lovers in the corner. These two had, at least since I arrived, been clutched on the window seat hand in hand, shoulder to armpit and frequently mouth to mouth. In one of their more accessible moments I heard the man bemoaning to the academic that since they had been together he and his love had been treated as socially undesirable. I waited to see the academic button down a grin, but he just nodded ponderously. So much for first impressions.

Out in the kitchen Sandi put me in the picture. The Parks and Reserves kid claimed the male side of the love-knot was a nark.

'How does he know?' I was quite impressed.

'They walk different,' she said.

'Like how?'

While Sandi was demonstrating a nark walk (crablike, with a head that shot from side to side), the science teacher pushed past us, tipped a couple of crumbled blueberry muffins off a small floral plate onto the table and tucked the plate into the pocket of her white linen jacket. Then she swept out the door. The academic shambled after her, mumbling and nodding.

Parks and Reserves came through straight after. He stood at the doorway watching them leave.

'Hey,' I said. 'That other bloke. How'd you know?'

He looked at me with pity. 'Couldn't you tell?'

'Not really.'

'When that stuff went round. You didn't see?'

'See what?'

'He didn't even inhale hardly. Just making the gestures, was all.' He threw his head back and snorted superciliously. I named him Rick.

'He was preoccupied,' said Sandi. 'It seemed to me.'

'See? That's what he wanted you to think.'

'You mean, they were just pretending?'

'Can you think of a better cover?'

I looked at Sandi. She was coughing into her hand.

'They'd've fooled me,' I said nicely. 'Most convincing.'

He smiled his Rickish smile. 'Hardly,' he said. 'They'd both be going on fifty.'

The lovers left soon after that. Perhaps they sensed he'd been rumbled. Parks and Reserves volunteered to trail them and no one tried to dissuade him. *Ah, youth,* we said to each other — us old ones who were left behind with the wine and an almost untouched bowl of strange-smelling dip.

Left to regress, we played music from Woodstock and *Easy Rider*. That was real music, we whispered to the ceiling. We smoked. We dared each other to taste the dip. We remembered places, movies, famous people. John's friend had been to

Graceland. He'd found it depressing. Tacky and pious and commercial, said John. I wanted to protest that what you saw there didn't count — it was the *going there* that mattered. But by the time my head had figured that out the talk had turned a couple of corners.

Afterwards the memory of Clive's party depressed me. There were five months between us. In five months I too would turn forty-eight. The only difference was, I knew better than to throw a party.

When I first met Clive, Sha was in her second year at school. I'd got a part-time job in a lunch bar. It was connected to a fish-and-chip shop where Clive worked in the afternoons. He'd dropped out of university the year before. All he knew for certain was what he didn't want to do with his life. We got to know each other by throwing questions and answers through the dividing door during quiet moments.

One afternoon as I was knocking off he said, 'Let's go dancing.' I guess I looked unenthusiastic so he told me it was his birthday. He had a girlfriend at the time. I thought they must have fallen out, and his birthday and all, so I said yes. I must've had someone around who could babysit. I don't remember all that. But I do remember the dancing.

It was a nightclub: a band, a bit of a dance floor and tables. I suppose we had a table, but I don't remember sitting down. Clive didn't dance like any Kiwi male I knew. He moved tight and certain, dark and fast. Like a Latin, I thought, going on hearsay. And he made it seem so simple that almost right away I found I could match him. When I ended a double spin his hand and mine were perfectly placed to meet. I could anticipate when he had in mind for us to shimmy apart and when to return. Our bodies were of a single mind.

After a time other people stopped dancing and simply watched us. When the music ended they would applaud. I was dizzy with pride and happiness. I felt like a doll on a music box, wound tight with adrenalin.

Sometimes, because we ended up right in front of the band, the singer's eye would catch mine and she seemed to smile at me. She had a strong, slightly graunchy voice and there was something straightforward about her. She looked younger than me, which seemed to be very young to be singing with such a capable band in such a sophisticated nightspot. I remember thinking that she was the only person in that room who could possibly be enjoying herself more than me.

On the way home, flopped in the back seat of a taxi, Clive confessed it wasn't his birthday. He'd just felt like dancing. In the years since we've sometimes said, 'Remember that night?' and vowed we'd do it again.

The singer that night was called Beaver. She had a solid career ahead of her.

If Sha was six, which she must've been, I would've been twenty-five. And it was winter, so Clive would have been twenty-six.

Clutching Hal in brown paper I went back to the alphabetical stacks in the second-hand record shop. BEAVER. Her picture on the cover, still looking straightforward. *Very Good $7*, said the sticker.

'Can't keep me away,' I said to the man at the record shop counter.

fourteen

You were crazy about him,' Spider's woman told her sister-in-law.

'George?' said Sha, thinking she must have misheard. Though they were sitting well back from the band because Spider's woman had sensitive ears.

Spider's sister smiled at Sha. 'George. True. I was too. I thought he was the cat's pyjamas.'

'They were living together,' said Spider's woman.

'Not really. Not quite,' said Spider's sister.

'He had his drums set up beside your bed.'

'He didn't have room in his place.'

Sha looked across at the stage, where Hal was scrimping words out between gritted teeth and the music was falling apart. Kevin had moved in beside George; he ran a finger across his throat, looking at Spider's back. Spider's womenfolk noticed nothing.

'I remember seeing you polish them even.'

'Okay. I was in love, I polished his drums. We all make mistakes in this life.'

Spider's woman grinned at Sha; she had the punchline. 'Then he shifted them to — '

'No,' said Spider's sister. 'That wasn't it. First they got a rehearsal place and he took them there. And we weren't seeing each other such a lot 'cos he was playing.'

'Around. That's what he was playing.'

'*That* George?' said Sha, pointing.

'That George,' said the sister, and turned to give a long soft look in his direction.

'George,' said Spider's woman, 'was a bit of a stickman in those days.'

The sister gave a little shriek at this lapse into filth.

'Well, he was,' said the sister-in-law. Then, to Sha, 'He had this other woman as well. Sarah.'

'Sandra. She was called Sandra. I ought to know.'

'And we all told you but you wouldn't believe it. It went on for months.'

'I thought George wouldn't do something like that.'

'Then one day she went round to this Sarah's.'

'*Sandra*, and she *invited* me round. That was the thing. It was deliberate. She showed me her bedroom and there beside the bed was his drums — the whole bloody set.'

Sha didn't find it as funny as they did but she smiled to be polite. It was the kind of story Kath enjoyed — angst and masochism turned sugary with age.

The bouncer with the shaved head was waving at her from the doorway. He pointed towards the office and cupped a hand over one ear. Sha nodded back and told the women she had to go.

He was waiting through the door. 'A few teething problems,' he said, of the music, trying for tact.

'One or two.' She felt he was holding her responsible.

There were still more people coming in than were leaving. They'd been playing about half an hour. She picked up the receiver. 'Willie? Where are you?'

'Whangarei. Got a lift. No planes till the morning. How's it going?'

'What happened?'

'The worst. Well I's remanded again. You wouldn't believe it. They're going ahead on the Class A and the lawyer's still saying I've got no case so I oughta plead guilty. So I said a few things. I said the lawyer wasn't on my side. Then the judge threatens me with contempt of court. So then it turns out their analyst witness has gone off for a piss or something and the judge says he can't waste any more time and remands it. It's such a set-up. They're all in on it, I see that now. I've had as much as I can fucking take, I tell you.'

Sha could think of nothing to say into the silence. She supposed he was crying. At the rehearsal that afternoon they'd been talking about Willie's Miscarriage of Justice, making it into a joke. Sha too. It was hard to take it seriously, to believe that while the rest of the country went on with their daily lives Willie had been singled out for meaningless persecution.

'Willie,' she said tentatively.

Two girls, Sha's age, walked passed the office. 'The fridge-freezer,' said one, 'has a twelve-month warranty.'

'Sha,' croaked Willie, 'I've done a bit of a terrible thing. I direct credited this to your mother's phone. I couldn't find a public phone and I had the number and so.'

'That's okay,' said Sha, 'she won't mind.' Willy's father owned half the country. Had Willie forgotten the number or what?

'Tell them I'm sorry I didn't make it for tonight. They got Julie okay?'

'Spider Brown.'

'Who?'

'Some old friend of George's. They had a vote and he was a bloke.'

'How is it?'

'Sad, pretty sad. They need you, if that's any consolation.'

'Sha, do something for me? Look after my Fender, and the amp's mine, make sure no one fucks off with the amp.'

'What are you saying? You'll be here.'

'Can't, Sha. Got to get out while I can.'

'Out where? Hey, you can't just...'

'It's not my fault. I'm sorry, tell them. I'm sorry but it's not my fucking fault.'

'You should tell them. I think you should come down and —'

'That's what they are banking on, for Godsake.'

'Who? Who's banking on?'

'Them. I gotta be a jump ahead of them, you see. At least a jump —'

'There's only another week, Willie.'

'So George's mate can stand in.'

'You haven't heard him, Willie. They're gonna be real slutted, Willie.'

'Let them, then. You're the only one I'm gonna miss, Sha. Only one I trust, you know that?'

'I gotta tell them you've fucked off? Me?'

'Sha, this is costing your mother a heap —'

*   *   *

Sha went up the back where people were standing. The Piano Tour Band were playing something Sha had never heard before. Something *they* had never heard before. Spider was singing. He was hunched before the microphone, looking ancient, wispy and nicotine-stained.

All God's animals are true-ue-ue...

Hal was punching a single high note. Kevin grinning like a madman.

... believers.

'You a reporter or something?'
'Yep,' said Sha. He was the heavy type, jeans pasted on like Gladwrap, short fair curls, know-it-all mouth.
'Critic? Who for then?'

Soon He'll be asking are you-ou-ou...

'Rolling Stone magazine.'
He stepped back for another perspective, uncertain. 'Where's your notebook?'

... a believer?

'Think I won't remember a performance like this?'
He laughed and Sha was ashamed of herself. She looked over at the stage and felt a wave of pity for Hal. The way he was keeping his face averted and slamming out petulant notes. Sha edged off into the crowd. It had become her habit to spend part of each performance among the uncommitted, the solid drinkers, the latecomers who stood at the back. Hal liked her to eavesdrop and report back. Sometimes she invented conversations to make it more interesting, but she hadn't invented the woman in Wellington who'd told her friend, shouting above one of Willie's convulsive solos, that she'd slept with Hal in '74. Twice. And it wasn't that great.

There were others from time to time who hung around after the show. Hal, remember me? Remember you said, and we went, and I said? Old girlfriends and one-nighters. Old all right. Some looked almost as tired as Kath. Nice motherly women who'd smile indulgently at Sha. She found it deadly depressing. Like the wrinkles on Hal's eyelids when he was sleeping.

She liked him best from a distance. Standing in the dark watching his hands, their control and absolute conviction. His voice. His face when he sang, which became something more than just a manface weathered by too much late-night living. Something sensual and complete. She was in love with the pianist. She was in love with the singer. But the man who slept beside her in motel beds had the eyelids of a man who was ready to settle down.

The longer they were together, the more Hal seemed to want her around. The more they toured the more Sha enjoyed life on the road. She'd got to hate sitting next to him in the bus. He'd look too long at little old houses by the sea, or crane around to talk to George about the flavour of free-range eggs. Worse, he'd fall asleep and expose his ominous eyelids.

Sha had smelt freedom. Having finally wrenched herself from the sloppy comfort of home and Kath she'd had an entrancing whiff of the possibilities of independence. She wanted to close the door to her own room in a boarding-house full of strangers — that being the loneliest act she could imagine. What she didn't want, not yet anyway, was a beach house, brown Leghorns and a domestic man.

When they took a break she joined him in the shadows beside one of the speakers. 'You look like a black stick insect,' he said. His arm went round her shoulders. 'I can't believe they're staying round.' He was staring out at the crowd. 'I can't believe this whole fucking thing. What are they saying out there?'

'Nothing much. They're speechless.'

Kevin brought over a flask of rum and handed it to Hal. Sha watched him pour it down his throat.

'George is feeling pretty bad,' offered Kevin. 'I dunno. I mean the guy wasn't that bad this afternoon. Least he was trying to play the same stuff as us.'

'Jesus Christ,' said Hal, looking past Kevin's head.

Spider joined them. 'Well,' he said, shaking a smoke from a crumpled pack, 'they're not running out the door.'

'Don't have to,' said Kevin. 'We've stopped.'

Sha had to cover her mouth with a hand.

Spider stared at Kevin then decided it was a joke. He smiled, looking at Hal. 'I thought you came in there really good. No one minded, did they? Just, I'd been working on a few songs, you know, in my spare time. Makes a change. Girls said it went down really well where they are. Change of mood and all.'

'That's for sure,' said Kevin heartily.

'I thought, in the next bracket maybe we should —'

'No,' said Hal.

'I thought maybe just —'

'No. N O.' He leaned over Spider shouting, 'Jesusfuckinchrist man, that wasn't music that was —'

'There's Christians here,' roared Spider. 'You realise there's Christians here?'

'Then give the poor bastards their money back,' yelled Hal. 'I felt like walking out. Only any minute now Willie's gonna come in that door. Any minute.'

Sha had to shake him by the arm to make him listen. 'He rang. Willie rang. He's still up north. He's not coming back.'

She knew she should've saved that till later but she couldn't stop herself. She was so agitated by this new, unmellow Hal. Somehow it felt as if this moment had been sketched in back when the Ol' Piano Tour was being planned.

Sha was keeping inconspicuous down the end of the bar. Cosmo brought a stool and sat beside her. Kevin's girl, Debbie, was with him. They were, both of them, looking serene and sparkle-eyed.

'We got taken outside,' he said.

'I'd never've guessed!'

'Strong as. Local stuff. Strong all right. Didn't even know the guy.'

Debbie climbed up onto Cosmo's knee and sat with an arm around his neck. 'Yeah,' she said. 'Good shit.'

In other circumstances the invitation would have been to Hal.

The crowd had thinned right out and Sha could see across to Spider's women at their table. She'd thought about rejoining them but it would have been taken as a serious breach of diplomacy.

With nothing for it but to get through the night they were playing better now. Hal had taken over and was howling out

117

blues, bleak and angry. Spider's guitar had been turned down, and now he was just tagging along and flashing smiles at one and all.

'You decided yet?' Cosmo asked Sha. It was a conversation they'd had off and on.

'Yes,' said Sha. 'It just came to me. I'm going to be a consumer. I think I have a natural bent for it.'

'Ah-huh,' said Cosmo.

'*I'm a man*,' groaned Hal. And they stopped clean, except for Spider. Sha clapped hard. So did Spider's women. Debbie kissed Cosmo just above his T-shirt label.

Spider stepped to the microphone. 'Friends,' he said, 'brothers and sisters, have you thought about Jesus?' And the next thing Kevin was there beside Sha taking a handful of Cosmo's tufted hair and turning his face the better to punch. And Debbie was screaming and people were pushing back to form a circle, and the bouncer with the shaved head was shoving his way through.

'HE thinks about you,' said Spider at the microphone. 'HE thinks about you all the time.'

fifteen

The windmill turns slowly. Close up it's menacing; an ugly pragmatic construction. Feargal Sharkey walks beneath the windmill. He climbs stairs. He is alone. He is accompanied by others. Feargal Sharkey is a pale tragic figure hunched in an overcoat. It never happens to him, he laments. Meaning love.

There are faces. Pale Anglo-Saxon faces withered and bleached by poverty, clustered together in family groups. It never happens to them either. Life, love, happiness passes them by. They are the cold dry creekbed; the water has forged a new channel across fresh green land. The camera grieves for them. It grieves for mankind.

I watch this scrap of film over and over and each time it makes me want to cry. It's as if something has reached into my soul and taken a smear for testing. I feel painfully, wonderfully mortal. I feel *interfered with*.

Also I overidentify. It never happens to me either. Or hasn't for a long time.

Clive's friend John lent me three tapes he'd made from *Radio with Pictures*, circa Karen Hay. We were talking music videos at Clive's party. Some I could recall, still, with terrible intensity. The young woman with the voice that reverberated through her nasal passage. A sound as lonely and treacherous as ice. A gold stud on her perfect nose and autumn leaves falling. Or Joe Cocker, a balding grocer with advanced Parkinson's disease and the charisma of a kitten, playing Joe Cocker. Husking it out at some mafioso club where the young Sicilian roosters strut out a fragmented drama of betrayal and revenge. Don't we know they are civilised men? Or Willy de Ville, exquisitely evil in all his camp decadence.

I am in love with men on video. With Bob Marley's tired, gentle cheeks. With Mark Knopfler's calm. With Mick's calculated elegance and Jimi's ruffled shirts. . .

Most of all I am in love with the late Lowell George in one dazed and mesmerising video clip. With the rest of Little Feat, making love long distance. A simple piece: they sing, they play, they appear to be semi-conscious. The music is organic; tendrils reach into the brain, into the heart. Lowell George sweats. He sings tenderly into the grey foam-covered studio microphone, he appears to be about to lose his balance and fall from his stool but he never does. Occasionally he smiles as if to himself. He seems totally unaware of the camera.

None of which explains why I am in love with this particular man in this particular video clip. There is not necessarily a reason. This video clip is one of a dozen or two that have moved into my head and are as personal and permanent as my own past. The people in them more real than relatives — I've spent more time with Keith Richards or Nina Simone than I have with any of my four cousins. That would only be a sad reflection on the times if I had splendid cousins.

To watch John's tapes I had to hire a video machine. I took it for a week. For the first few days I played it constantly, turned up loud so I could hear it in the shop. I got seven approving comments and two complaints. Nobody ever remarked on my playing the National Programme. I think they didn't even notice.

The remarkable thing about the tapes was that John's selection reflected almost exactly my own preferences. There were very few clips that didn't please me. Besides: no commercials and a fast-forward button — what more can anyone ask? Very few were entirely new. I had watched them with Sha on Sunday nights five, maybe six years ago. An indulgence, for she had school next morning. Even then we were setting a pattern.

At night I sat up late watching. It felt decadent, cocooned. I had got into the way of believing it was necessary to be plugged into the world, to hear the news, to watch *Foreign Correspondent* and the least absurd dramas; that therein lay the guiding rail to sanity. Without such things I felt precarious and adolescent.

On the third night, during Bette Midler, Willie arrived. Not wickedly wasted Willy de Ville but Willie of the Ol' Piano Tour. He stood at the door with a guitar case under his arm. His hair had been cut very short; he looked temporary, like a young soldier on leave. I peered behind him, waiting for Sha. I thought I'd confused the tour dates.

He held out a five-dollar note folded lengthwise. 'I owe you for a toll call.'

I wanted not to hear Willie's convoluted story. I'd turned down the sound on the TV but my eyes kept sneaking to the screen. To the Cure, at once bizarre and cosy like a little old lady's ouija board. To a small boy dancing to Van Morrison's Celtic-dawn music on a band rotunda in a chill Northern twilight. To the Legionnaires' diseased and edgy touch of vampirism...

On the bus to Auckland Willie had come up with a scenario he could believe in. He refused to accept the more plausible explanations; that the police had been looking for a decent conviction to justify some desk-dreamt operation, that Willie's refusal to give them useful leads had seemed a wilful naughtiness that required punishment, that some cops are bent and/or malicious, that the legal system is capricious and inefficient and that everyone knows musicians are constantly drugged to the eyeballs.

Willie couldn't believe it was that haphazard; that it could have happened in fact to any young man travelling in the company of other men and apparently having a good time. 'It's traditional,' I told him. 'Goes back to the gypsies. People were stoned to death for less.'

'That's quite good,' he said. 'Quite clever. *Stoned.*' He was treating me with deference because I was his friend's mother.

In Willie's version everything had been orchestrated. The Drug Squad lads had gone north with a copy of the Ol' Piano Tour itinerary and ten grams of heroin. The object was to nail William Crowley and thus render his father, Duncan Crowley, vulnerable.

'To what?' I said.

'Blackmail . . . revenge . . . ruin.'

'Who'd want to do that?'

'Anyone. Someone who hated my father. Someone with influence.'

'He's a hateful man?'

'That's not the point. He's really rich. That means powerful.

121

If you're rich you have enemies.' Explaining carefully because these were difficult concepts for a friend's mother to understand. In fact it was the most coherent I'd ever heard him.

'Crowley, Rouse,' I suddenly realised. 'Your father's bought this building. He's going to knock it down.' Willie's eyes explored my flat. He didn't bother with sympathy.

'In that case,' I said, getting back to the point and my suspended scepticism, 'shouldn't you tell your father?'

'I can't.'

'Won't.'

'Can't. Physically can't. If I was to stand up now, intending to go there and try and explain . . . I couldn't. My legs wouldn't do it. I couldn't make them move, not one step. Besides, that's what they want me to do. That's why it's taking so long, they're waiting for me to go to him.'

That's when I was watching the solemn little schoolboy dancing on the bandstand to Van Morrison's music. The beauty of it. The simplicity.

I said doggedly, 'But if . . . this person . . . wanted your father to know he would have made sure it was reported in the city papers.'

'I thought of that. There's a reason. They want to be sure I'm convicted first.'

I tried to tell myself all this was no more unlikely than the events that had befallen Willie. 'There must be someone else you can go to?' Other than me. He wasn't listening.

'I won't be convicted. That's the point. I'll shoot through, they won't find me.'

'Shoot through to where?'

'Sydney, I guess.'

'What about bail?'

'My own surety. They can't find me, they can't make me pay.'

'What about your mother?'

He gave me an odd look then turned away. We both watched Van Morrison and his small friend walking away along a winter street.

'Willie,' I said. 'You go to Australia you'll need a passport. You'll be in the computer. They'll pick you up. Wouldn't it be easier to just turn up in court?'

'Passport? Oh shit.'

He sat for a while with his face turned away. I thought he was crying. I wasn't sure whether a hug from a friend's mother would be any help. I wasn't even sure why he was sitting in my living room telling all this stuff that had nothing to do with me.

Willie said, still not looking my way, 'I didn't tell Sha, but this cop tried to tell me it was Hal that dobbed me in. Shows how low they are.'

I was shocked. 'Why would he say it?'

'Just to cause trouble. That's how they get their kicks.'

'You don't think that it might be. . .?' I had this sickening need to scratch at the idea.

'Get the lead guitar player arrested? Last thing he'd do.'

'Willie,' I said — it had been on my mind all along, 'you don't think maybe they did find the stuff? In the motel? One of the others. . .'

It was a betrayal. His face said so. Still I kept on. 'Were you sharing a room? So, who with?'

'Hal.' He said it with such finality, as if there was no further room for argument, as if he'd said 'God'. He looked back at the TV. Stevie Ray Vaughan in a red jacket, his cigarette smoke dancing. 'Okay if I turn that up?'

He fell asleep during the last tape. I woke him and sent him off to Sha's room. I lay awake besieged. What should Willie do? What would I do if I was Willie? Could Hal have? Did Willie intend to leave or had I lost a daughter only to be landed with a son? Would Hal? Might Willie's theory be right? (If so, how sheltered and comparatively sweet life was for those of us at the other end of the economy.) Crowley of Crowley and Rouse! I knew what he looked like even; the man was always in the press, passing lofty judgment on hyped-up issues of no great concern. When would they reply to my letter? And could it be more than coincidence that Willie had come here? Was Willie acting on instructions?

Already I was living dangerously.

About Second Gear: I'd talked on the phone to someone from the Legal Advice Centre. She told me I should get legal advice!

123

I rang the law firm that had handled my lease. I didn't identify myself. I talked to the office girl, asked what the hourly rate was. She said, icily, that she couldn't give that kind of information on the phone. I was enraged. It's just a service, I told her, same as a plumber.

I dragged out my old Olivetti, an enormous leaden machine, and rang Clive. He told me to think of a figure and double it. I rang Rose, who now had an interest in my property dealings; she said think of a number and treble it. The number I thought of was $18,000 which was what I made last year before tax. The tax consultant told me I could be investigated because Inland Revenue never believed anyone could live on less than $20,000. Last week, he said in tones of wonder, his wife had paid one hundred and fifty dollars for a pair of shoes. I told him to send her to Second Gear.

. . . prepared to accept in consideration for the breaking of the lease agreement the sum of $54,000. . .

If I snickered just typing the numbers however could I expect them to take me seriously?

. . . prepared to accept in consideration for the breaking of the lease agreement the sum of $36,000. . .

ONO. . .

John and Sandi had called in with the tapes while I was working on the letter. He said I should be a bit careful, those kind of people didn't like being messed about. If I upset them I could find myself getting beaten up by an intruder or falling off the harbour bridge. I looked at Sandi and she wasn't smiling. John owns a tow truck business. I turned up the roll bar so he could read what I'd typed. He straightened up and laughed at my fearful face. 'That's petty cash,' he said, 'to the likes of them.'

John would believe Willie's theory.

I started a new letter:

. . . for the breaking of the lease agreement the sum of $38,000. . .

No reply.

Willie ate five Weetbix for breakfast, with milk and brown sugar, and told me about his revised plans. He would go somewhere and live in the bush until it all blew over. He would eat fern

124

roots and shoot wild pigs and practise acoustic guitar. He would wait.

I watched him spooning the soft mush into his mouth which was too small for the rest of his face. He looked like a flounder with little dark eyes where the spear had twice stabbed. Not a handsome young man, but the world has got bored with handsome; ugly has more clout.

I contrived an instant video of Willie eating Weetbix at my kitchen table; hard-edged white-trash ambiance... relentless close-ups. It would end with Willie walking out the yellow doors of Second Gear and raising his hitching thumb to the seething morning traffic. Youth. Futility. Waste.

'I think,' I said as I drained the teapot, 'I've got an idea.'

sixteen

On the ferry Hal was recognised. After a time of looking and whispering the three women came over. They told Hal they just loved his music and one got his autograph on the cover of her chequebook.

Hal behaved beautifully, as if this was a rare and precious moment in his life, though it happened quite often in public places. He introduced Sha. He told a story about New York. Of hearing Muddy Waters and sitting at the next table to Dr John's.

Sha hadn't heard this before. To her he never volunteered stories about his past, though sometimes things could come out when she was talking about someone famous. Like Eric Clapton. *Met him?* Several times.

At that moment on the ferry she was feeble with love for the autograph-signing Hal, the singer, the man who played piano and had touched the stars.

What had he done wrong? Why wasn't he in Mozambique or Biafra with a documentary camera crew trailing behind? Crouching beside a row of living skeletons, wearing a distinctive hat and a famous-person-confronts-the-unimaginable-enormity-of-man's-inhumanity-to-man expression. Why wasn't he on Coca-Cola ads? Or touring the world on behalf of elephants or trees or advertisement-free Sundays? Why not a Living Legend, humbled by success? Why Elton John but not Hal Barber?

Sometimes he thought there was a definable factor. Willie had it. Something to do with focus. Of not seeing beyond or around your music. Obsession maybe. The world way in the background, unreal. Willie would get to be rich and famous. Could, anyway.

But Willie was rich already. He might be short of cash but the money was there in abundance. And possibly fame wouldn't mean a lot to Willie because of the world itself being out of focus. Anyway, who needed it? Not Hal. Except for the sense, sometimes, of having come close but never quite got there. He'd have liked it to prove things to other people; the boys who tortured him in the primary school playground, his long-lost sister Barbara. And perhaps to Sha. If he was terribly famous he wouldn't feel this humiliating need of her. She had broken him, as mindlessly as a baby dismantling a doll. A skinny pseudo-Gothic kid with no perceptible talent except for the ability to hold up a head weighted with half a tonne of metal earrings.

On the other hand Hal was a bit famous. In fact he had never quite stopped being surprised by his own success. He could have been a garage mechanic in Cambridge or a real estate salesman in Turangi. He could have been a bum cadging coins from tourists. None of those eventualities would have surprised him as much as his real life did.

He was professional. That was a matter for pride. He was reliable. He delivered. Didn't throw scenes or lay trips. He worked at a club, the management would always want him back. Now, on what could have been his final tour, he'd fucked up. Last-minute cancellations of everywhere south of Christchurch.

So there *was* nothing south of Christchurch. A few tinpot towns and Dunedin, where they had their own style of sound and didn't care much for outsiders. But it was still no way to end. And without a decent ending he had nothing to build on. Bloody Willie. What was the bet he had the smack on him? Young enough, dumb enough to give it a try. Or maybe not to use, but to sell. Raised to make a buck regardless. Could it be that some *instinct* had prompted Hal into naming Willie? Better the lad had a good fright now than a life on the needle. Fair to say, then, that Hal had done Willie a favour. And in return Willie had fucked off, left them in the lurch, limping home in a stinking old bus, tails tucked under.

Except George who took the first flight home to be with Annie and the kids.

Contentment. Does it really feel good at the time? Or only

when you look back on it?

Sha came to lean against him. They were on the Desert Road heading north; Hal was driving and remembering the horses. They'd charged right across the road, running in a pack. His father stopped the car. No one owned them — that's what stayed in Henry Head's memory of the horses. They belonged to nobody.

Sha smiled at Hal. She had these moments of affection if ignored for long enough. She was wearing Cosmo's headphones. Hal reached over and pulled them from her ears. She gave him a benign stoned smile and carefully transferred them to Hal's head.

Hal was hurled into a tunnel of sound and brutally assaulted. It was Armageddon. It was the aftermath. It was mankind with a bloody rag between its teeth and fifty thousand watts sizzling the neurons. Trash metal... speed metal... whatever. Plutonium, more like. Compared to this stuff Meat Loaf was Mrs Twiggletoes and AC/DC would be in short pants forever. This was the sound that had turned suicide into a positive option, or so it was said. Play the tapes backwards for the totally shocking bits, so the sillier tabloids claimed. Could just mean that backwards the words can be heard as more than a screaming vocal death-rattle competing with guitars. In any case, what words are able to shock when *kill* is frayed with overuse and *motherfucker* is just another macho endearment! Pity the kids, hungry for outrage in a world that's long past taking offence. Satanism at least still gets some people going. But death is the one truly effective gesture of contempt.

They'd kill you for saying it, but a generation earlier and these same kids would've been listening to Elvis, Little Richard, PJ Proby, Alice Cooper. A whole tradition of outrage, then somewhere in the late seventies it went tame. On the surface, that is. In reality it just went underground. Heavy metal, being the fastest, meanest music around became even faster, even meaner. So the radio stations and the TV music shows wouldn't touch it. That being a recommendation in itself — this stuff is BAD music.

Hal watched the road up front as it began to wind gently

between red-brown tussocked hills. A holocaust was playing in his head. Kids strolling around with their brains under siege from strobe sound. You saw them everywhere, walking in the sun with their ears plugged to Walkmans. Secret sounds in their head, high-voltage adrenalin. A religious experience, why not? Frenzied internal voices; someone getting through to them. If not prissy old God it must be the Prince of Darkness. Ooo-eee.

Sha was tugging the earphones off his head. 'Good, eh?' He couldn't tell if she was serious. She didn't switch the tape off. The music raged, emasculated, from the earpads. 'Still,' she said, 'it accounts for Cosmo.'

Hal barely smiled.

'What d'you reckon?' she asked him.

'I think,' Hal pretended to himself that round the next corner there'd be a bunch of wild horses, 'I think I'm glad I'm not seventeen. I mean where the hell can it go from here? What's left?'

'The *explosion*,' said Sha and smiled affectionately as she fixed the earphones above the several used-car parts that hung from her lobes.

No one sang on that long ride north. No one even strummed. Kevin and Debbie rolled about in the back seat in a passionate conspiracy, from which Debbie would occasionally disentangle herself in order to parade the four steps up the aisle smiling at Cosmo and doing little aerobic stretches. If he raised his head Cosmo would look right through her. When he wasn't reading comics or rolling joints Cosmo pretended to sleep. His fingers would sneak up and touch his bruised and swollen mouth.

Hal drove all the way, hunched over the wheel. He seemed to be ignoring Sha, which made her nervous. It was as if, despite her better judgment, her life had been making unspecified plans which might include Hal, and now they were in jeopardy.

Without George and Willie the bus seemed empty. A couple of times Hal stopped to pick up hitch-hikers; two German girls, then a madman who sat jabbering to himself. They all got off at Bulls although the German girls had said they were heading for Auckland. Might have been the atmosphere, or the passive smoke that Cosmo was blowing about.

Willie's amp and guitar were safely in the back. Sha had double-checked. She was pleased that Willie had entrusted her. People didn't usually give her responsibility; she didn't inspire confidence.

Mostly Sha stayed in the same seat staring out the window. Cosmo would call her over from time to time to share a smoke. Always loud enough for Kevin and Debbie to hear. He never offered them any, though he knew they had none of their own left. The rift was *that* bad.

Sha felt sorry for Kevin but not for Debbie. Being fought over had been the silly cow's great moment. Later she'd wanted to share it with Sha — *Kev said, Cos said . . .* Sha gave her a look that said *What are you?* — a look no friendship could survive.

When the tapes finished Sha turned them over, rotated them. They pounded their frenzy into her brain. The sound of eternal motorways. Like drowning in an ocean red with blood. The words — those she could make out — didn't match the ecstatic overreaching of the guitars. An experience. As music she could take it or leave it, but one thing was clear; after hearing just what was out there, she couldn't go home. Not to *live*. Her and Kath, the way it was, in that dark little outhouse of a flat, stuffed with stockpiles of shrunken cardies and mentally retarded suits.

She rang Kath collect from Taupo. Five seconds and they were arguing. *Please don't shout.* 'I'm not shouting.' *So must be a new thing they've invented to magnify your voice.* 'Ha.' *Willie came here.* 'Yeah? How was he?' *I'll tell you about it when you get here.* 'Tell me now.' *When you get here, I said.* 'For God's sake.' *I presume you're planning to stay?* 'What's that supposed to mean?' *It's not supposed to mean anything. It means, shall I air your bed? It means, the two of you or what?* 'I suppose the two of us. Just for a couple of days or so though, while we sort things out.' *What things?* 'Just things, for God's sake. I'm not coming back to stay, Mum.' *That's fine.* 'Do you have to sound so wounded?' *Wounded! I was trying not to sound too relieved.* 'You did a good job then — "that's fine"?' *Will you be here for tea?* 'I've no idea. It depends. If we are we'll get takeaways, okay?' *Okay.* 'How are you, anyway?'

Just south of Bombay Hills Cosmo reclaimed his Walkman.

Thoughts of the future accosted Sha's silent mind. Lumbering, heavy shapes that refused to leave. She went up to the front and stood beside Hal. He glanced at her and nodded. Sha needed to ask questions and make statements but her tongue was unwilling. She felt sorry for Hal, who was just a man like anyone else. A man like anyone else was not what she needed, not yet. She placed her hands at the base of his neck and kneaded the flesh. His hair was speckled with grey. He smiled up at her. Her tongue freed up a bit and she told him Spider's sister's story about George who used to be a stickman. Only she said 'ladies' man' because suddenly Hal felt like a stranger — full of interesting possibilities, and she didn't want to seem crass.

seventeen

They were tired. I made allowances. I made coffee and toast. They were tired, but there was more to it; the minute they walked in and dropped their bags beside the door the very air stiffened and twitched. Sha plonked herself at the table. Hal mumbled a few polite remarks in my direction and sank into the sofa. They were out of each other's line of vision and too stuffed to turn their heads.

I overcompensated. I smiled. I chatted vacuously. I boiled and browned and buttered. I couldn't be certain that those edgy vibes weren't coming from me. I turned grotesquely maternal and distributed playthings. To Hal his own record. And it worked. His jaw fell open. He examined the cover on both sides.

'Shit Kath, havvenseentinyears wedgagetit?'

'Take it,' I told him, 'it's yours.'

He protested a bit. Could be a collector's piece. Some of the old Kiwi stuff was worth a bit now, at least in the US for some reason.

I insisted. I'd removed the price tag. He was entitled to his optimism about the value, but the man in the second-hand record shop surely knew better.

'Should I put it on?' I asked.

Hal glanced towards Sha then shook his head. He laid the LP on his knees and sank back into relapse.

To Sha I gave my manuscript. She glanced at it bleakly and began to flick the pages, counting.

'So what is it?'

'Something I wrote,' I said. Regretting it already. Rigid with embarrassment at admitting I wanted to *do* something, *be* someone. Is there anything in the world quite as squishy as poor saps whose hopes outstrip their talents?

'It's an essay,' I said. 'An article. Something. About Elvis Presley.'

She studied the first page. 'You want me to read it,' she said in a voice of distress I knew from the past. *You want me to make the bed. You want me to sweep the floor/bring in the washing/set the table/exhaust myself!*

'Doesn't matter.' I went to snatch it back but she dodged my hand.

'I just want to know — what's it for?'

'It's for me, that's all.'

'Ah.'

'As a matter of fact I thought I might write a book.'

Her mouth twitched. 'About your *life experiences*?'

'About you,' I said. 'It'll be a cautionary tale.'

She seemed to make an effort to read the thing. Turning one page. Then another. Hal's eyes were closed. The coffee was in the pot but not yet poured. I spread raspberry jam on the toast. I tried not to watch Sha. Her opinion suddenly seemed ridiculously important and final. Eventually she looked up.

'Tell me about Willie.'

I gave her a look that said, not here — not now. We both looked at Hal who still had his eyes closed. Sha sighed and went back to my faltering first steps into the vibrant world of literature.

Hal woke as I set out the mugs. At least he opened his eyes (remembering what the cop had told Willie, I could no longer take the man on face value). We sat around the table and Sha dripped butter on my manuscript, wiped it off with the sleeve of her shirt then pushed the thing out of harm's way. Hal rallied enough to tell me about their last night in Christchurch — the roadie punching up the bass player and the stand-in lead guitarist who was hot to convert. He had a way of telling stories that kept you wanting more. Even Sha laughed from time to time. That fiercely upright hair on top of her scalp would shiver. It had grown some, her hair, and changed colour. Purple splotched with peacock blue.

A bit later she took my Elvis piece and left the room. Hal was running out of stories, or inclination. I struggled to throw words into the silences. With Sha gone these had begun to feel dangerously intimate. I could hear myself breathing. I could hear Hal breathing. I was close to reading a significance into the fact of us both having lungs. And I'd thought I was over all that — had *worked it through*, as they say.

Sha called to me from her room. Divine intervention? I trotted off geared up for praise; you wouldn't *summons* someone in order to heap shit on their best efforts. Their creative impulses, as the lady in the TV ad says. Sha was sitting on her bed. 'About Willie?' she said.

'Clive's been left a house by the beach. Across the harbour. Up from Waiuku. And Willie was talking about going to live in the bush. He has this idea he's caught up in some heavy stuff to do with his father, I dunno. Anyway we took him down there, me and Clive. And he said to tell you but no one else. He's a bit odd, seems to me. They're gonna catch up with him sooner or later.'

'This place—can you draw me a map? Can I borrow your car?'

'It's a long way. And the starter motor's dicey. Sometimes you have to get under the bonnet and push the little button.'

'How long to get there?'

'Two hours, maybe more.'

'So what's the time now?'

'You can't go tonight.'

'I can't stay here. I mean, nothing to do with you, I mean it's really nice to see you and all that but. . .'

'What is it,' I said, 'with you and him?' I knew she'd hate me asking like that; confronting her. Sha preferred life to be all nuances and vague shadows of meaning.

'I don't know.' She was bellowing like an injured calf. 'Can't you see I don't know.'

'You and Willie?' I prompted helpfully. 'That it?'

Her look said, 'Are you a cretin or wot?'

'Friends,' she said carefully, as if it was a complicated word I mightn't have come across. 'I'm looking after his Fender.'

I had a vision of Sha draped across a polished chrome bumper fighting off a crazed spare-parts merchant. I sniggered. She stared at me hard, then fell backwards on the bed and rolled about a bit. 'That's not remotely funny,' she said, clutching her knees.

'I know,' I spluttered.

'It seems ages,' she said eventually, 'since I had a decent laugh.'

'You've been mixing with men — what can you expect?'

She followed me back into the main room. Hal was back on the sofa, his mouth hung open. Sleeping for sure — the pose was too unflattering to be pretence.

'I have to go,' Sha said with certainty.

I looked at Hal. 'What about...?'

'You don't mind?' It was a plea.

'If it won't start you have to open the bonnet and...'

'I know.'

'About your Elvis thing,' she said, 'I think it's quite good really.'

I handed her the keys to my car. She put them in her pocket, then she grinned. 'Weren't you lot real rebels, eh?'

Hal woke not much more than half an hour later. I was at the table ironing a blue cotton skirt. I told him Sha had been called away by a friend who had some emotional trauma. I made another cup of coffee. I felt artificial and clumsy and was angry with myself. Hal began to pace about the room. It was full of obstacles. We dribbled some inconsequential chat. Eventually he insisted on taking over the iron and thumped his way through several garments. I remember myself explaining inanely how a bit of ironing made all the difference between rags and wearables.

He finished the ironing and looked at my clock. It was after nine. 'Feel like a drink? We've got an hour.'

'I've got no car.'

'The bus is outside. But why not walk?'

Gluepot. Bottom bar. Seemed I had a lot of friends. Even people I knew very vaguely were coming up to chat. Seemed he had even more friends. There were even three or four people we had in common. *Didn't know you two knew each other!* Not once did I say, 'Well actually Hal and my daughter...' I just smiled and let them jump to conclusions.

The hour was galloping by. Hal's friends included a couple of locally famous people. They also included Sam, a short gentleman of the cool-dude variety — all sweaty charm and studded black leather, who wanted to take us to a party when the bar closed. Hal looked at me over the top of Sam's head.

'Why not?' I said.

Sam stood on his toes to smack me a kiss on the cheek. 'Good on you, man,' he cooed.

Squeezed in a corner of the back seat, Hal's arm, of necessity, around my shoulders, I nursed the paper bag of rum and Coke. We passed through suburban centres I'd never set eyes on. From time to time Hal's spare hand would fumblingly transfer to mine a damp roach, feebly glowing. The air in the car was harsh as a dragon's breath. There was debate, I remember, about whether a window should be opened. Unknown voices declaiming in the dark. 'Man,' said a voice I knew to be Sam's, 'we'd be spewing out smoke like a bitch on heat. There'd be cops zero in from all over.'

We were cowboys. We were outlaws.

Sam wasn't the driver. We seemed to be travelling steadily and straight. I hoped *that* much had changed in the years I'd been behaving like an adult. A taxi home, I promised myself.

The party was in a double garage at the end of a concrete drive which ran past the house. The roller doors were opened up and people spilled out and stood around under the stars. There was a band in one corner of the garage, two men and a woman, dreadlocks and the happy, homely sounds of reggae. There was a reason for the party. Someone had reached twenty-one. We met her. We met everyone. Sam toured us round making introductions. He seemed so proud of us. He seemed so proud of them. Hal and I were smiling at each other over his head, just from the pleasure of being there.

Large sections of the night disappeared. Sam and I danced. He was neat and fierce — elbows tight at his sides, body jack-knifed, he stepped out some methodical routine of his own. We returned to Hal but I hadn't the courage to ask him, so I joined a young woman who was dancing alone. Sometimes our eyes would coincide and we would laugh for no particular reason. Then I danced with the uncle of the girl who was twenty-one. It felt like that night with Clive. We were attuned, uncle and I. We couldn't put a foot wrong. We beamed at each other with this secret knowledge. We waited for the next tune. Then the next.

The music began to change. Old rock singalongs ... 'Proud Mary', 'Get Back', 'Brown Sugar' ... everyone joining in. Hal had been dragged to the band corner. He sang. I suddenly thought of Sha who might be home and wondering.

The house was open and busy with people. I asked the woman nearest the door if I could use the phone. She took me through to the living room. A very old woman and a girl of perhaps thirteen were watching TV. I dialled and waited. If she was asleep would she appreciate being wakened to be told we were at a party?

The girl said, of the old woman, 'This is her favourite programme. I taped it for her.'

I turned to look at the screen. I kept the receiver at my ear. It was that thing where they find missing people and get them together with their friends or relations. I'd only seen it once. I'd seriously thought of writing to ask if they could find Lil of Johnny Ray fame, but the prospect of cameras put me off.

My phone went on ringing. I began pleading in my head for her to answer. I was suddenly thinking *accident* and seeing my little blue car crumpled in a gully beside the last lonely winding stretch of road. No phone where Willie was. I wished I had risked her resentment and demanded a few specifics regarding her plans. Five more rings. Four. Three. Two. One. Minus one. On the TV screen there was a photo of a boy who looked just like Hal. A bad sign. Please God extract me from this before it's too late.

I put the receiver back in its cradle. 'Who was the kid in the photo?'

'His sister wants to find him. They had her on just before. She lives in the States.'

'What was his name. Did y'hear?'

'Henry,' the girl said, pleased with herself. 'Henry Head.'

See. An obsession.

'Also called Hal,' said the old lady in a voice that was astonishingly deep and definite.

He was playing the mouth-organ, an anguished lonesome-road sound. People had stopped the jokes, the kissing and the boogying in order to listen. I stood among them, so impressed, so grateful. I thought, this is why musicians are so feverishly loved; they bring the rest of us such pleasure. And, whatever their reasons for making music, we the audience see it as an act of generosity.

They were having a good time, Hal and the band. They could hardly wait to finish off one song before storming into the next. There was no chance of talking to Hal about a boy in an old photo.

The older people had begun to leave. Uncle demanded one last dance. We hugged each other goodbye. I went up then and stood close to the band. They had their heads together, playing odd notes, looking for something else they all knew. Hal wheezed out the beginning of the Battle Hymn of the Republic. The guitarist and the bass player looked at each other, shook their dreads.

'Amaz-i-ing grace,' I sang by way of suggestion. The guitar player echoed the notes. Smiles. Hal reached for my shoulder and drew me in towards his microphone. People were waiting for me, they flashed encouraging smiles. I felt like a baby in a roomful of aunties, being encouraged to take my first steps.

Amazing grace how sweet the sound that saved . . . Look at me, Sha. No hands. Watch me . . . *a wretch like me-e-e.* I can I can. *I once was lost . . .* All listening, watching me, and I'm not terrible at all . . . *but now I'm found . . .* I can do it. I'm okay. Hal smiling. Drummer smiling. Sam pushing to the front . . . *was blind but now I see.*

Afterwards I got embarrassed. Hal giving me a universal grin, the bass player asking what else I knew. Some instinct telling me to get the hell out before I ruined a perfectly perfect night, so I wriggled out between players and leads and stands and found myself a dark corner. Sam came over and stood beside me. 'Man,' he said, 'you sure made some ba-aad music.'

'Sam,' I told him. 'That's the nicest thing anyone's ever said to me.'

In the taxi home Hal and I pooled our cash and counted it, holding the notes up for identification in the sneaking streetlight. What's wrong with me that I find men with cash-flow problems so attractive?

He'd started talking about Sha — about how alike we were;

same expressions, same mannerisms. 'Last time I was at your place,' he said, 'it freaked me out a bit. The two of you like some trick that's done with mirrors.'

'You were staring a lot,' I said. We were travelling fast into dangerous country, serpents and crocodiles. I half-hoped Sha would be waiting there to save me, then I thought, it's too late, *this* is the sin, what happens beyond this is irrelevant.

He looked away from me out the window. 'I do that,' he said, eventually. 'It's my gimmick.'

Daylight was beginning as I waited on the pavement outside Second Gear while Hal paid the driver. No sign of my little blue car. Hal came and stood beside me, put a long arm around my shoulder and we looked at the dawn reflected in the windows of the Designercraft arcade. *Thank you life, for this.*

'Scuse me while I kiss the sky.

After Johnny of the Rockbusters and before Steve of the mermaid eyelashes there was another musician. He played acoustic guitar, folk and classical. By day he worked in an advertising agency and Saturday nights he played and sang songs of peace and protest in a coffee bar. I thought he was a faultless human being and I expected to live with him forever. I wanted him to be the father of the children I was going to have.

He was happy when I became pregnant. Possibly he became less happy as my body became lumbersome but I didn't notice. By then I had left my job and in order to bring in more money he began to take guitar students in the evenings. Some came to our place, others he went out to teach. There was one called Miss Poole. He used to tell me things about her . . . how her glasses would slide off and land on the strings as she played . . . her china cat collection . . . the terrible cocoa she inflicted on him every time.

One day I answered the phone and an irate man asked if he had the guitar teacher's number. I said, yes, but he was out.

He said, 'I'm Angela Poole's father — does that mean anything to you?'

I said it didn't but somehow already I knew.

'The Tuesday night pupil,' he said.

Then I knew for sure — quaint old Miss Poole was Tuesday night.

'She's sixteen,' the father said. 'She's a child. What kind of monster is he?'

'Are you sure?' I asked.

'Lady,' he said, 'we understood she was taking lessons at your place — till a friend of mine saw them booking into a hotel for a couple of hours. A couple of hours! What kind of cheap thing does he think she is?'

When the guitar teacher got home we had words. He said he couldn't help it, the sight of my swollen belly was so distasteful to him and Angela Poole was so young and lovely.

I put some clothes in a bag and caught the train home to my mother. I stayed with them for the first few months of Sha's life. I've told her, 'Your father played acoustic guitar and he was nearly as skinny as you.' Nothing else.

I never saw him again, not even in the distance crossing a street.

We sat, Hal and I, on the back step in my ugly little yard and the sun came up on us. I needed nothing more than that. I wanted much, yet I was content with the way things were. There was definitely life after motherhood, after GST returns, thigh wobble and economic restructuring.

Words came and went, small straight waves without undercurrent. Hal wanting to settle down, house by the beach, studio work, perhaps teaching keyboard (*uh-huh*, I thought), the life he'd been living was just protracted adolescence. Growing old, he said, without growing up. In the seventies he'd bought a section at Piha. He could borrow and build. Or he could sell and buy a place somewhere undiscovered. Soft dreams. Easily, I could have slotted into them. Another opportunity shop did seem, by comparison, to lack vision.

I fetched a rug and cushions as the sun stretched to the lawn. He talked about music, about electronics and audiences who got younger all the time. I saw then that the age-gap between us was significant, that he took it all for granted. Whereas those of us who were pre-Presley, and can remember what a bleak time our ears had of it — well, as the old soldiers say, who can describe it? You had to be there.

Dangerous comments surfaced in my mind from time to time. *Willie thinks you shopped him. Sha is with Willie.* Surfaced and dived again, as alien and inappropriate as a submarine.

I must have been the first to fall asleep, my face against his shirt, his piano-playing hand placed over the back of mine.

When I woke from that damp discomfort of sleeping in the sun I could smell coffee and hear the all-day roar of traffic. Hal was singing. On his record he was singing . . . *ain't no substance bends the mind like love. . .*

He came to the door where I was hugging my own stiff bones. The sun was mid-morning. People would be peering irritably into the shop for signs of life. I didn't feel too bad about that; my customers were the kind of people whose lives were built on disappointments.

He returned with coffee. 'It's not bad,' he said, of the record, sounding surprised. 'It's not at all bad. Did you listen to it?'

'A lot,' I said.

He sat beside me. 'Are you hungry?'

'No.'

'Neither am I.'

Suddenly I remembered the boy in the snapshot on the TV screen. I began to tell Hal.

'. . . looked like you. Not exactly, but around the mouth.' He was watching me with a slight, pleased smile. It occurred to me that he thought I was betraying my state of mind.

'. . . girl said his name, which was . . . shit, you know I've forgotten. But the surname was Head. I remember that because. . .'

'Was it Henry?'

'You know I think it was. Henry. Yes. Then this old old woman. . . It *is* you. Hal? For real? You?'

He rang the TV people. They gave him a Wellington number. 'Go on,' I said, so he rang that.

I opened the Second Gear doors and fastened them back. No one was waiting. There was a carton with a giraffe's neck printed on it lying in the middle of my doorway. The milkshake snaked right across the footpath and ran into the gutter.

eighteen

'When you think about it,' said Willie, 'it makes sense. All the real crazies — the ones that go loose with knives or axes and wipe people out — they say they did it for God. They were *told* to. There's a terrible lot of bad things going on in the world and most of the worst of it's done by people who have this, I dunno, *relationship* with God and everyone says they're crazy. But what say they're telling the truth? What say God's finally cracked up and turned into a raving lunatic? No one seems to have thought of that.'

Sha was trying to get at the baked beans inside a tin that was speckled with rust. She was using a knife and a block of wood she'd found by feeling about in the long grass under the tank stand. Willie seemed to have lost interest in eating once he'd finished off whatever Kath had been thoughtful enough to provide when they brought him out here.

'Do they?' said Willie.

If she hadn't been so hungry, Sha would have seen the funny side. She had expected to find Willie bound up in his own problems and here he was theorising about insanity. The wood missed the knife handle and bludgeoned her thumb. 'Shit damn Jesus Christ,' she danced with pain. Willie watched her until she came to a stop, thumb still in her mouth.

'See,' he said. 'Even you associate God with violence.'

She thought about going home immediately. She had come to see him, she had brought the Fender, enough was enough. She might even be in time to catch a late-night takeaway at Waiuku.

But the long drive on her own at night had been more daunting than she'd expected. Besides, she hadn't left so suddenly on Willie's behalf. She was escaping Hal; the need for decisions, having to commit herself one way or another; the sense of something intangible but *awry*. And from Kath's compulsion to have things *aired* . . . identified . . . folded away.

Willie was standing at the French doors. 'You haven't seen the beach.'

'I can smell it,' she said, nursing her thumb in the palm of her right hand. 'And one beach is very like another, especially in the middle of the night.'

'There's a moon. There's a bit of a moon. And you can put your thumb in the water, the best thing for it.' He picked up the acoustic guitar as if it was the obvious thing to take to the seashore.

She followed him down the wooden steps that led from the verandah to a sandy track that ran from the house to the water. It was a very short track. From the house you could look out at the sea. It was the sighing black space between the bottom of the section and the distant stretch of electricity that was Auckland. Sha had driven in a safety-pin direction. If some vast earthmoving thumb squeezed the pin shut, Wattle Bay would be swallowed by concrete overpasses and throughways.

The water wasn't cold. Sha thought about a swim but it seemed to involve a vast amount of effort. She let the surf froth around her feet and soak the bottoms of her tights as she drowned her thumb. It throbbed anxiously. It struggled, then went limp. *I'm a thumb murderer*, she thought.

Willie had stood for a moment on the wet sand looking across at that wild light, then retreated to sit on the stones and pluck soft sounds on the guitar. When she went up and sat beside him he said, 'A song, a really good song, can last forever. Have you ever thought of that?' All the time his fingers kept moving about the strings as if of their own accord.

'What d'y'think of that speed metal?' said Sha, but Willie was off again.

'It can just soak into people and be handed on generation after generation until it's just part of *existence*. Imagine that!'

Sha was getting impatient. Ever since she'd arrived Willy'd been coming out with these stupid little wisdoms. She wanted to shake him, to snatch the guitar and hurl it into the night. *C'mon Willie, get real!* She couldn't do that. It would be too much like her mother. But Willie was acting like just being at Wattle Bay was some kind of solution. Like he had more important things to think about.

'My mother's worried about you,' she said. Perfect approach. 'She thinks you're not exactly facing up to the situation.' *Twing twing twu-ung.* 'F'rinstance money? How're you going to manage? If you apply for the dole you'll be *on record.*'

Thunk, his hand closed round the neck and choked off sound. 'Tell her not to worry,' he said.

Sha ground her heel among the pebbles. 'What about *your* mother?' she asked.

'You *know.*' He sounded angry.

'Whazzat spos'da mean?'

She ran off with the decorator. It was in all the papers.'

'When was this?'

'Years ago. When I was six. It was in all the papers.'

'Why was it in all the papers?'

'My father was a millionaire already. And he was — you know — always asked to comment on things, bit of a mouth. Well *you know.*

'No,' said Sha. 'I'm not much interested in rich people. It's a bit like reading about *aliens* — like I don't really expect to meet many so reading about them's kinda boring.' Then she thought she may have hurt his feelings so she tried to make it reassuring. 'I know your father's a big wheel etcetera but I think you might have a kind of distorted view of how interested people are in someone like that. I mean wives run off all the time. It's not exactly a *scandal.*'

'He was a dwarf,' said Willie. His voice like a finger probing a wound.

'Don't be a bigot.'

'It makes a difference,' insisted Willie. 'Whatever you think, it makes a difference. The papers made it into some kind of joke.'

'Yeah,' said Sha. 'I think I do remember something. So what happened?'

'My father married this woman and they had a couple of kids.'

'You don't get along?' She could hear herself, just like Kath, sniffing around for certainties . . . something solid enough to hang explanations on.

144

'Get along?' He sounded contemptuous, which was strong for Willie. 'What does that mean? Gettalong? Shit.' He planted his feet on the stones and stood up in one movement. He walked down to the soft sand then stood, looking back at Sha. She got up as she was supposed to and joined him. It was so easy with Willie; no need to check her exits, score points, be on guard. She joined him and they walked together at the edge of the water.

'I've been listening to Cosmo's tapes,' she said. This subject seemed to have become an obsession.

But Willie was talking at the same time. 'Your mother doesn't believe they didn't find that shit in our motel.'

'You know mothers.' *U-oops*, she thought, *tactless*! But it seemed he wasn't even listening.

'She told you about the cop? Saying it was Hal?'

'What was Hal?'

'Told them. I was into. . .'

Something clicked into place in Sha's mind. She tried remembering the motel room in Kaikohe, the mess of it, Hal's face. None of the images were clear.

Willie was getting steamed up, his walk had turned stiff and bolshie, he swung his head from side to side as if he was in pain.

'Maybe he did,' said Sha. 'He was there on his own till my bus got in. Maybe it's true.'

Willie swung round. 'Wha. . .' he said. He was furious. 'Get real, Sha. What would Hal wanta fuck up his own tour for? See, see, see,' he was hugging the guitar to his chest, 'even you. Same as the others. You wanta believe those bastards. You see what kinda power that gives them? That's what I'm up against. Even you, Sha.'

He spun round and began to walk back the way they'd come. She stood and watched. Half way up the beach he turned into a black swooping bird. She ran a few steps and saw he was swinging the guitar around in wide arcs as if he was about to toss it into the sea. He wouldn't. She was almost sure he wouldn't.

She looked away, staring out across the water at that vast spread of lights. She felt bad about Kath, about having left in such a hurry. Kath was a bit of a worry. However you looked at it she didn't seem to have much of a future. And nothing to show for the past but Sha and great piles of disgusting old clothes that anyone of sound mind would cart off to the tip. If only she'd go and live with Clive, which was the obvious thing; they could watch TV and keep each other company. They could be *middle-aged* together. That way Sha could stop feeling compromised and *snatched at*. That was it, Kath had nothing to replace being young, and Sha was her way of feeling in touch with *what was going on out there*.

But what *was* going on out there? Sha wasn't clear on that at all. Too many years of living at home with Kath. Nineteen, and she'd thought Exodus was just the last chapter of Gideon's whatsit. Kath had dictated their music . . . films . . . books. Not *meaning* to — she was always asking Sha's opinion, the *youth* angle. . . like the stuff on Elvis Presley; what can you say when the real question is *who gives a shit? The man is DEAD in every sense of the word*. How many teeny-boppers are scribbling off letters to pop magazines saying . . . *Elvis is so freaky. He is ABSOLUTELY my all-time fave at the moment?*

There was Kath, fixed in her tight world of the shop, the odd movie and a little group of friends, thinking Sha was her window-to-the-world. What she didn't see was that there was something so absolute, so *definite*, about her world and her opinions that any contribution Sha might have had was suffocated before it even had time to take shape.

When Sha looked again for Willie he had disappeared. She walked slowly back to Clive's bach. Her arms felt cold in the sea breeze.

Willie was not there. In the only bedroom there were two bunks. He had been sleeping on the bottom one, there were a few old grey blankets. Sha helped herself to a couple and climbed to the top bunk. The ceiling was too close to stand up.

She considered the evidence against Hal and found him, in all probability, guilty. Motive and any mitigating factors she disposed of as irrelevant. It was an inexcusable thing. It was age and authority turned against youth. She was pleased to find that for once, concerning Hal, she could feel decisive. If it turned out the drug cop *had* made it up she was going to feel, in a way, cheated.

*   *   *

146

When Willie woke her it was well into the morning. He seemed cheerful. He had managed to open the baked beans. Furthermore he had heated them and they were served.

Sha had been having one of her warning dreams, in which she was always about to stumble into a pit or off the edge of a nine-storey building. She couldn't remember which kind it had been, but by comparison Willie, sunlight and the hiss-thump of waves seemed altogether beautiful.

The baked beans were so gruesome they could've strayed out of the dream. Sha sat opposite Willie, spearing at them, wanting to be grateful. Her fork had two prongs crossed tightly, as if it were holding its bladder. The beans fell apart as soon as they were approached. Revulsion made her suddenly clear-headed. She must get away from here and eat some decent food and return Kath's car. And she couldn't leave Willie here, he was obviously incapable of surviving.

'Last night,' she said, 'I was thinking about those cops, that they can't be allowed to get away with it. Whatever the reason, the fact is they set you up. Bet they do it all the time and it's gotta be stopped.'

Willie's face was so grateful. He was being *believed*. He kept nodding while Sha paused to work out where this was taking her.

'That's the main thing,' she said, giving herself more time, 'they have to be *shown up*.'

Willie looked disappointed. 'They never are,' he said mournfully. 'They can't be. That's the point.'

'The right kind of lawyer, they could be,' said Sha.

'Cost.'

'Willie,' said Sha, imitating Kath's boring friend Miriam, 'if you went to your father, what is the worst thing that could happen?'

Willie thought about it. 'He could be killed,' he said.

'Why?'

'I don't know, do I? 'Cos I dunno what's behind it.'

She put a piece of bean between her lips to give her strength. 'Willie, if someone wanted to kill your father they'd just go ahead and kill him. Let's try and be real here, shall we? Anyway, I didn't think you liked him.'

Willie looked shocked.

'Okay — what's the worst thing etcetera *apart* from that?'

'He'd lose money.'

'That would upset you so much?'

'It'd upset him.'

'Let's try "the worst thing that could happen *to you*?" '

Willie thought about it for some time. Sha was summoning up saliva in an effort to swallow the small lump of orange mush in her mouth.

'He'd make me get a proper job,' Willie said.

'Doesn't approve of musicians?'

'Depends. The ones who make a lot of money he approves of. That way he can see the point.'

'You're what, twenty?'

'Eighteen.'

'No shit? Eighteen? Still, that's of age.'

'You don't know him,' said Willie miserably.

She smiled at him. 'Why not be a rich musician?' She shoved herself over the table towards him with sudden eagerness. One hip bone scraped through her plate of mushy orange beans. 'I'll *manage* you,' she said. 'You won't be just an ace guitar player, you're gonna be a phenomenon. Different sound. None of that old good-time rocker stuff. You're gonna be off the edge, gonna play that way, gonna look that way. You've gotta be faster, freakier, more psychotic than anyone else around. Willie de Ranged! Bringing the word that God has finally flipped out.'

Willie had gone from surprise to cautious interest. 'What would you know? About managing?' he said when she ran out of words.

'I just do,' she told him. 'I'm the ultimate consumer.'

She slid back, spreading baked beans across the table. Some splodged onto the floor. She felt ablaze and, for the first time ever, absolutely confident.

She said to Willie helpfully, taking over already, 'Would you like me to come with you to see your father?'

Willie stared at her, trying to look with his father's cool blue eyes which would see a Munsters character in a black outfit that didn't so much resemble a garment as a piece of cloth she'd rolled around in for several days before fastening it to her person

148

with ribbons and safety-pins. Reinforcements of which were stored on her earlobes. Flame-coloured porridge dripping down one flank.

'P'rhaps not,' said Willie.

nineteen

$15,000. Or in other words, fifteen thousand dollars. The man offered and I accepted. I knew even as I stood there, nodding like a bull with delirium tremens, that my friends would tell me what a fool I was. Should've pushed him up . . . he would've expected . . . the way it's done . . .

I knew all that. I knew too that fifteen grand was peanuts to the people who drove past my shop all day in their brothel-creeping cars. A couple of weeks' salary, a quarterly bonus, one-sixteenth of what they lost in the crash without even hurting, except maybe their pride. I knew all that. Miriam and Tom had struggled their way into that mind-set, even if they didn't quite have the income to back it. When I was with them I felt obliged to pretend eccentricity; I *want* to be a poverty-ridden shopkeeper living in a dingy lean-to out the back; it panders to my woolly concepts of social justice. And maybe I did. Maybe it did.

As Tom once pointed out, if I *minded* the way I lived I would have found ways, *seen* the opportunities, to change it. On the other hand, Tom had not tried being a woman who raises a child on her own. And being one of those is something. Not exactly the fast-track to becoming *renowned*, but something nevertheless.

Over now, though. Done. Reassessment time.

So there was the man saying *fifteen* and me going *yeahyeahyeahyeah*, but not such a bunny that I was prepared to sign beside the pencilled X. 'When you bring the cheque,' I said.

'I called by earlier but there was no sign of life.' He gave me an infant-school teacher's smile. Bad girl, don't deserve a gold star (but I'll let you have it just this once).

'Had an emergency.' None of his business, but it was a knee-

150

jerk reaction; money is power. I happened to look down at the floor of the shop. He had walked through the milkshake. The sole of his left shoe had stamped my floor (*four weeks to be out*, his document stated) with little yellow crumpet faces. Yet two worn-out ladies were already piling their arms with items to be dragged on and off in the fitting room. *They* had managed to look down and watch their steps.

Next thing the imperious people from the mall would be over complaining. Of course I should have been out there and sloshed water. I had intended to but I was in a state of serious malfunction, not even thinking about minding the shop, but acting out some necessary role in a clichéd morality play. A *musical* morality play, this one, and I was trying to be gritty and unassailable . . . some kind of Patti Smith . . . with my own life to get on with when I knew — oh yes I knew — I was really some treacle-clinging Crystal Gayle or Tammy Wynette, stomping out bugger-you lyrics that were never meant to fool anyone. Brave-face-on-broken-heart territory. And sure, that kind of stuff's despicable. But sometimes, have you noticed, it kind of creeps up on you when you're not looking and it *touches* you. And it feels, at least at that moment, like THE TRUTH.

I watched him leaving — Santa Claus Hargreaves — and of course there he went, so chin-up that he was paddling in banana thickshake and still never noticed.

I forced myself to sit down for a while until the urge to run out back and throw myself upon Hal . . . *take me, I'm yours, I'm randy and I'm RICH* . . . had passed away. But by then another idea had taken root, even come with a tune. *You got a section down in Piha/I got the money to build* . . . Never had so much been conjured out of so little. The odd thing was when we were together I'd felt I had it all under control. Now he was a room away and I was falling apart. Money gives you expectations. I was ready to blame Sha, for being my daughter, for having left us alone. 'Forbidden' is a fierce aphrodisiac.

I left the ladies browsing. Let them turn into sneak-thieves stuffing their bags with used bras and emptying the till, what was a bit of petty cash to me? I realised then that this . . . *windfall* had a darker side. It was money-for-nothing, the first to have come my way. Not courtesy of indiscriminate luck, fairy godmother Lotto's wand falling from the skies into my bewildered but deserving hands, but *through the system*. Unearned money — in olden days it was inherited along with the estate and membership of the gentlemen's club, but in the eighties the yuppies discovered a new kind, or maybe created it. Either way, it made working for money so old-fashioned, so *anti-progress*, it was contemptible.

The unearned money came from buying things, waiting a bit and then selling them for a great profit. Sometimes these were tangible things but more often they were abstract numbers on pieces of paper. It wasn't so much a method as a spiritual philosophy, so although it wasn't foolproof even those who lost out remained adherents. What else could they do? Because what they'd learned as members of the faith was that you were either up there with the unearned-money makers or you were one of the rest who were all, unwittingly, contributing towards that glorious golden fountain of unearned funds.

Well that was my economic analysis. Tom was right in a way. It wasn't that I'd chosen to be poor but that the only route out of poverty seemed to be to scramble up there to cloud nine. And something scratchy and ill-defined — *honour?* — had seemed to stand in the way. It's a historical fact that the mugs have always been morally right. That seemed quite important.

Past tense, notice. Bought for a handful of silver without even a thought for the wider implications. But what alternatives? Let them keep the money? Give it to charity?

Forget the wider implications. *Take it take it take it, why not?* Already I was thinking like a yuppie.

Hal had tidied the kitchen, put away the dishes. I could hear the washing machine shuddering in the horrible little alcove that passed for a laundry. He was watching it with suspicion.

'Is this normal?'

'Afraid so.'

'Hope you don't mind?'

The plastic basin was empty. My knickers were in there soaking bloodstains but now. . . I have no clothes basket, he would need the basin to carry the clothes into the yard. The man was going on forty, it can't have been his first encounter with bloodstained knickers.

But a mother-in-law's bloodstained knickers?

'I thought Sha would've rung,' I said. Apologising for her; an instinct — her faults are my fault.

'She's avoiding me,' he said. He seemed quite happy about it. I waited for a little more, a crumb of explanation such as you'd feel obliged to offer a friend. The machine gave its last orgasmic shudder and sighed to a halt. Hal began to unload it.

'My sister's coming over,' he said, not specifically to me. 'Twenty years I haven't heard from her. Thought she was dead. Shit. Imagine.'

All I felt was put-out. *Bitch*, I thought, *twenty years and you have to wait till now.* I could see the night before . . . Hal, me, and possibilities that kept seeping into my unguarded mind, all dribbling away. God knows I wasn't foreseeing a future for us. But then again. . . *She's avoiding me*, he'd said so cheerfully. And Sha: *I can't stay here.*

So I didn't share my news. He was all fired-up about his big reunion. Tears of joy to be shared in the nation's living rooms. . . perhaps that pleased him. . . a good reunion a boost to his career. And I would watch, oh avidly, nothing would stop me.

'Going down town,' he said then, clutching the basin which he'd piled high with wet washing. Looking faintly guilty. Anything I needed? It wasn't till he'd gone I began to see it his way. Stranded with this woman he barely knew, no home of his own to go to, waiting for a girlfriend who seemed in no hurry to return. Situation like that, even renown mightn't be of great comfort.

Hal left, Sha arrived. Neither had planned it that way, but it may have been for the best. She was wound up and noisy. It was early afternoon and I had five customers — *possible* customers — in the shop all at once, which was the most I'd had since they'd started revamping our end of the street. She started off telling me about Willie's father's house.

'Fucking mansion. Should see it. I mean it was way up in the distance, behind this great bloody park. Through the trees. I dropped him at the gates to the park. He wouldn't let me drive up. Should see it. I mean fu-uerck, what a place.'

A woman, one of my regulars, marched out clipclopping as

loud as she could. I gave Sha a look, but even without my impending closure I wouldn't have cared too much. The woman was strictly a 50-cent forager — never went near my charming creaseless bargains on their racks.

So Sha had talked some sense into Willie, but had also taken on board his tendency to leap to conclusions. 'Hal,' she said, all black and flashing with outrage, 'dobbed him in. I mean fu-uerck. I mean can you believe.'

I kept my voice to a surreptitious murmur, making a point. 'I thought that was just cop talk. That's what Willie said.'

'Willie!' said Sha in a megavoice which at once celebrated and lamented Willie's unworldliness. Then she turned fragile, 'What if it's true?'

Sha and the four remaining customers were waiting for my reply.

'It can't be,' I said with such conviction, I surprised myself. 'But what if it *is*?'

'You can't *what if*. There's no point unless you know.'

'But. . .'

'And even if it was true — well, he might have had good reason.'

My daughter's mouth fell open. She was staring at me as if my tongue had turned forked and black. And for a minute I thought she *knew*, she could read my stupid heart. But as she turned and stomped towards the door of the flat — even her back was cutting me dead — I understood: all her growing life I had been the dispenser of principles. We may have been short on possessions, but mother was always full to the gills with moral certainties: equality, liberty and taking your place in queues. And now, suddenly I was slip-sliding on one of the bigger ones; not dobbing people in.

The money not even in my hand and already I had changed.

She slammed the door behind her. Three of the customers were still taking an unabashed interest. I gave them an *ain't that the way* look and trailed off after Sha. I knew they'd approve. People in a hurry seldom shop at the likes of Second Gear, and one was a mother and one was a daughter and one was a potential shop-lifter; each was willing me to go out back and follow it through.

I let Sha go first. 'You're starting to think like an old person,' she said. 'D'you know that? Few years down the line and you'll be campaigning for them to bring back hanging. You know what it is, don't you, Willie's young so he's wrong and the cops are right.'

'Cops seem pretty young to me. Most of them.' I knew it was a feeble defence.

'The *system*,' she said. 'They're part of the system and you believe in that now 'cos it's people your age are running it.' She leered. 'All you old *rock 'n' roll rebels*.'

'You had to be there,' I wanted to say. But I'd seen the old Ed Sullivan clips, the hordes at Woodstock; history had turned us into a joke.

Sha wasn't through. 'You're out of touch,' she said, not unkindly. 'All your lot. You don't know what's happening out there, how would you, you don't *go* anywhere? I don't mean the movies or a meal, I mean *socially*. No one old does, hardly.'

'Because,' I said, '*socially* everyone's under twenty-five, and deaf.'

'*See*,' she said. 'You sit in front of the telly and see what's happening in other countries and believe *that* 'cos it's somewhere else. What makes you think it's different here — that judges aren't silly old drunks, and cops don't lie and everyone's not ripping everyone else off? Because they don't show it? Wise up, mother. It's people your age that run the TV. They're as blind as you are.'

Shit I was proud of her. My daughter, all right. All this talk about the young these days being simply on the make, no motivation, no social conscience, no *rage*. I stood there humbled, yet at the same time — if you'll excuse the expression — *redeemed*.

'Who's minding the shop?' Sha said. 'Or have you gone self-service?'

The rest of the afternoon I fretted about the money. It began to feel like an imposition about to be thrust upon me. I mean what did I *need*? (A video, a decent pair of black pumps, a new shop . . . should I look at *buying* a place? That terrifying leap into the world of mortgage and maintenance. . .) And wasn't it beholden on me to take the money offered by a greedy industry? Willie's father's company's money.

What if Willie's father wasn't prepared to step in? I had a wonderful idea. I could help. I could use the money to fund a lawyer who would be fearless in his exposure of chicanery. The case would be a warning, a blow struck for the young, my show of faith.

Hal must have come in the back way. When I'd shut up the shop — an hour early due to my state of health — he was out the back with Sha. Some musical apparatus sat in my living room.

'What's that?'

My ignorance caused brief amusement. 'An amplifier.'

'It's Willie's,' said Sha. 'I'm looking after it.' She grinned. I knew she was remembering the Fender even though it hadn't been funny.

I got the impression Hal hadn't been there long. One of them had brought in the washing — Sha I supposed, since it was folded, my knickers in a pile of their own. She sat at the table stabbing a ballpoint at a piece of paper. He was on the sofa. They were sharing one of those bruised and dumbfounding silences that come with non-negotiable love.

It was a lesson to me. This time I saw beyond doubt that the man was fixated. When he looked at Sha he was like a heading dog eyeballing a stubborn old ram; poised to chase, guide, devour.

So last night was just a night out dressed up in foolish illusions. I was so grateful there had been nothing to everlastingly regret. Beyond that I felt only exhaustion and a sharp yellow pain in my head warning me that the last two aspirins were wearing off.

I made myself busy, dissolving analgesics, boiling water, opening and closing cupboards. I gave some despairing thought to dinner on behalf of others. I couldn't remember back to yesterday when food was something to look forward to. I wondered if we might all toddle off to Anton's, or even just the Chinese takeaways. I didn't consult. The silence told me it would be presumptuous to plan for a future that was at least two hours away.

'I feel wretched,' I said. Announcing it too clearly, like I was playing the maid or nanny — some walk-on part in the People's Playhouse annual production. 'I feel wretched. I'm gonna have a lie-down.'

As if this was the cue she'd been waiting for, Sha said, just as clearly, and almost as unnaturally, 'You shopped Willie.' Looking at Hal.

I forgot about the lie-down. This was my little Sha who was never, ever forthright except to me, who didn't count. Sha who hovered clear of decisions and confrontations.

Hal's heading-dog eyes flicked across at me, than back to skewer Sha. 'Whedju get that?'

'Cops told Willie. You did, eh?'

Hal put his head forward. The fingers of his left hand combed up through his hair. He rested his forehead on the palm of his hand. Sha kept staring at him. She was trying to stop her face from crumpling up into tears. I looked at her and thought *what now*? And I thought, *what good did it do? What's the difference? What does it matter?* I could hardly believe it was my own mind, dredging up stuff like that.

Hal pulled away his hand and stood up in one movement. 'I don't have to defend myself against shit like that,' he said, looking at the floor somewhere between Sha and me. He began to stride about gathering up his clothes and shoving them into one of the bags, taking his keys from the mantelpiece. Sha sat quite still, not watching, staring down at the sheet of paper where she'd set down numbers — 1, 2, 3, 4 — followed by spaces as if she was compiling a list. The way she was flopped in her chair, with her fountaining blue and purple tufts, she looked like a dead kingfisher.

I stood against the wall so as not to be in the way. Hal swung one bag over his shoulder and put the other under his arm. He glanced at Sha and I thought *surely* . . . But that was it. He stopped in front of me with his head jutted forward and low like a turtle and we stared at each other. And it seemed to last a little too long — as if his eyes were holding mine with both hands. He said, 'Thanks, Kath, for. . .' He touched my cheek with his fingers. 'See you round,' he said.

'Yeah,' I said. 'See you.'

He closed the door behind him.

'You could go after him,' I said.

The kingfisher rolled its eyes.

I was listening to hear the bus start up. Daft, it had been parked way down the side street and the groan of traffic was already gearing up to the late-afternoon crescendo.

'So he did,' said Sha in a flat voice.

'You still don't know.'

'Jeez-us.' She shook her head over my stupidity.

'Why then?'

'Whyddja think? Save his own neck is why. Save his own wrinkly old neck.' She was apportioning sides, me over there among the old and untrustworthy.

I wasn't going meekly. I sat myself across the table from her. It felt false. Now that talking to members of your own family has become high tech with instructions provided in magazines and bestseller manuals, it's hard not to feel like an emissary from a polytech counselling course.

I said, 'They're buying me out of the lease. And I thought . . . if Willie's father isn't prepared to help, or if he just wants to bury the whole business, then I could pay for a good lawyer, someone who'd show the whole thing up for what it was.'

She looked at me kindly, patiently. 'It's okay. That's very noble but it's okay. Willie rang just before, his father's got it all in hand already. They're gonna drop the charges.'

That *easy*. Was it naive of me to be surprised?

'But,' I said, 'dropping charges — that way nothing changes.'

'It does for Willie.'

'You know what I mean.'

'Mum,' she said patiently. 'No matter what, nothing changes. You just gotta see that and take it from there.'

I wanted to say, 'Child, child you are only nineteen, you know nothing of the world.' I wanted to feel able to say that with conviction, but I felt like the child. We've learned to both fear and respect our kids because they seem to have the world's measure.

I said, 'That's bloody terrible. It's *sad*.'

'But honest. At least it's honest. Your day you all ran around thinking you'd change the world, how *neat* you all were. But what's to show? You were just a bunch of phoneys.'

'Yeah?' I said. 'Yeah? You're so sussed then what're you gonna do with your life, I mean what does that leave?'

'Get rich,' she said. 'That's what it leaves. Though I've only just got to see it.'

'That's what I raised you for?' Pushing clichés. Words I despised rearing up out of some primeval maternal mist and leaping out of my mouth unauthorised.

Sha was unfazed. 'Deprivation,' she said, 'is the best grounding. Gives you that *edge*.'

'So I've heard,' I mumbled, then pulled myself together. '*Deprived?*'

She looked around. She let her eye dwell on the stained walls and the threadbare pseudo-Persian carpet. She smiled at me.

'We'll get somewhere nice,' I said, 'this time.' *We*, I thought, realising I had been in suspension ever since Hal came onto the scene, not really knowing if this was it; if I was or I wasn't . . .

Now it had turned out I wasn't. It was a kind of relief. I could feel my life slipping quietly back into place. Sha and me, another Second Gear, perhaps of a slightly more upwardly mobile nature.

'Kath,' she said, looking a bit strained, 'I won't be staying. I mean not for long.'

'Where. . . ?'

She wrote 'move' in the space after 1. She looked at me through a strand of purple hair. 'Somewhere a bit more. . . appropriate.'

'Right,' I said.

'Oh, for Godsake. . .'

'What?'

'I *knew* you'd be like this.'

'I said right. That means fine, okay, good on you . . . As long as I know. As long as you're sure.'

'You'll be okay?'

'I'll be great. I'll be fine. You think I'm senile or something? Chrissake, I'm only forty-seven.'

Which is no age at all, nothing. Just a place in the middle of nowhere. I knew what she was thinking: forty-seven and what's to show for it?

Only your good self, madam.

And my endangered principles.

'Whatever you might think,' I told her, clutching to the only wisdom born of those forty-seven years in which I still had some confidence, 'I believe that there is some kind of cosmic justice and on the whole people do reap what they sow.'

'Karma?' she dangled the word from one corner as if it was a used handkerchief.

'Something like that.'

She looked at me steadily, her eyes closing in with amusement. 'That's nice,' she said, 'I hope it'll be a comfort.'

After 2 she wrote 'tell lies'.

'If there are no rules,' I said, 'it doesn't matter whether he did or he didn't.'

She considered. She doodled a question mark at the bottom of the page. She grinned across at me. 'Yes it does,' she said. 'The thing about there being no rules is there's no consistency either.'

twenty

'You know,' the man said, 'Barbra Streisand... Da da da de *da*.'

'That's it,' said the woman. 'Perfect. God I love him — whatsisname — ooogh. They shouldn't make them so bloody gorgeous, it's not fair on us girls.'

' "The Way We Were", ' the man clicked his fingers, applauding his own memory.

'Us!' squeaked the woman. 'Sweetie, who are you kidding?'

'The name,' said the man. 'Da de da da DAH.'

' "Memories", ' said the woman, 'was the song. The movie was called *The Way We Were* but the song's called "Memories". '

'Even better,' said the man. He looked at Hal. 'What ya think?'

Hal picked out the notes to show he knew what the man was on about. The man smiled.

'Robert Redford,' shrieked the woman. 'I knew it'd come to me.'

'I'd thought of...' Hal doodled out the tune with a couple of fingers. The man was looking doubtful. 'Our Dad used to play it,' Hal said.

The man began to look much happier. 'Fine,' he said, 'okay. Perhaps there's some story?'

Hal did some judicious censoring. 'Not really,' he said. 'Except the piano was in the passage because it wasn't a big house but it had... you know those old T-passages? It was in the bit that led to the toilet. You had to squeeze past.'

The man was smiling, he clapped his hands together. 'I like it. What else?'

Hal pretended to be searching his memory. He didn't wish to be unhelpful but he had no intention of excavating his scabrous childhood in front of a couple of million viewers. 'He played mostly,

I think, when he was depressed.'

'Your parents separated, I gather.' It wasn't quite a question. Hal was jolted to think this man had got his information from Barbara. He still couldn't quite believe she was alive, that the woman these people were in touch with wasn't some bizarre imposter.

'That's right.' *Separated.* What a wonderfully normal sound it had! 'I was about ten at the time. Thereabouts.'

'Did you always play?' The woman's voice was oleaginous with respect. Hal flashed his teeth at her; the question was too silly to answer.

'Bit of luck as far as we're concerned,' said the man, 'getting a celebrity in our net.'

Hal held down a groan. The silly sod knew full well that *they* were the celebrities, that one meaningful smile on prime time provided more in terms of status than any amount of talent or dedication. Not that he envied them. Imagine making a living out of sitting in front of a camera being *nice.*

'You know you're our closing item,' the woman told Hal. They both kept assuming he watched the show and since he hadn't corrected them initially it was now too late. Still he figured that *last* was a compliment; Hal and Barbara were to be the evening's grand finale.

What a show he could have given them! His mother's grotesque breakdown, his father's shameful flight, Barbara and Hal on their own trying to keep things *normal* in a way that seemed, when he looked back on it, to have been in itself slightly unhinged.

Hal could imagine a family — George's family, since that was the one he'd most recently seen in action — chattering excitedly during the closing commercials. *But isn't it lovely, after all that, that they got together?* (Annie). *You never know, just never bloody know, what's going on in people's lives* (George). *If I went crazy would I go round being filthy? Heee heeeee* (Pita). *You must be, then, 'cos you be filfy all the time. Heee hee* (Tama).

Driving down from George's in the rental, back over the same roads he'd travelled in the bus barely a week before, Hal had considered *going nationwide,* as they say. Giving the people from *Reunion* their money's worth. After all it was *exposure,* which

162

was something the bastards hadn't been offering much of since Hal returned from his travels expecting . . . well, not to be *mobbed* . . . but at least to be an object of public interest. As it was, the only publicity he did get he'd had to drum up himself in a roundabout way through old contacts.

Logic had told him it could do no harm to roll back the blankets and display the family linen, no matter how sordid. He and Barbara were victims, scarcely more than children, objects for pity and perhaps even admiration. He tried to imagine himself telling the camera terrible secrets. . . in what manner? Bearing in mind his admirers, who would normally not watch this kind of show, but this time, because of the pre-publicity. . . Compassionate-but-wry sounded about right but already he was bunching up inside and he knew he couldn't do it. Not stand up and admit that's what you came from. . . that weirdness. Tarring yourself publicly with the same brush. He'd been certain Barbara would feel the same. And evidently she did. *Your parents separated.*

Hal tapped out the notes again, *Chat-ta-noo-ga Choo-Choo.* He said, 'Do you think I should just do it like that? A music-box effect, sort of teasing the memory, or play it for real?'

The woman nudged Hal's shoulder. 'I do believe we're a little excited,' she said. 'Ooo go on, you're allowed to be.'

Hal tried to ignore her. The bitch of it was, she was right.

The man was saying, 'They both have something going for them. You're the musician, what do you reckon?'

Hal picked out the verse. *Da de de da, dedade dada dade dada.*

'Start like that,' said the woman, 'and then slide into the virtuoso stuff. We've got to have a bit of the real thing.'

'That's the ticket,' said the man to the woman. 'Perfect.'

Hal had spent five days with George and Annie and the boys. The first day was good, being with George who understood about the tour, how cutting it short had been no less than amputation, that Hal was still *bleeding*, but would recover — being an old pro. Recovering . . . getting on with the next . . . that was what pros did.

In other ways staying with George's family was not such a

good idea, it rubbed salt into the wounds. They were like moss, that lot; spread secure and gentle on this earth, their lives were filled up with each other, their animals, neighbours, relatives, friends. And Hal could see he'd left it too late and that, anyway, Sha would have been all wrong for that particular solution.

They asked about her of course. Hal said it hadn't worked out. She was too old, he said, turning it into a rueful joke. Looking at Annie he kept telling himself that was the kind he needed. *Sensible*. Which meant at least over thirty. But could he *relate* to a woman over thirty? — sexually that is. His women had always been around twenty, they were the kind he got to meet, they were the kind he saw himself with, they were the kind he'd *always* seen himself with.

'Her mother was coming on to me,' he'd told them. It made him feel better.

'You didn't fancy?' said George.

'Christ, she's going on fifty.'

'How old are you, Hal?' asked Annie with a little smile.

'It's not physical age,' he said irritably. Thinking, that's exactly what it was. Loose flesh on the neck, little dark rivulets trickling into the eyes. Each time he'd looked at Kath closely it'd given him a shock because in other ways she was so much like Sha and he associated that with smooth-fleshed desirability, with *youngness*.

Kath had seemed to be made up partly of her daughter and partly of Hal. That was it. He had felt both attracted and repelled. Yet he had also felt at ease with her, like he was floating in warm water. As long as he didn't look close.

Before he left George's place news came through on the grapevine that Willie's old man had got the case dropped. Hal felt . . . not so much absolved as righteous. 'If he'd done that in the first place it would've saved us a lot of shit.'

Annie said she could understand why he hadn't wanted to. It couldn't be much fun being that man's son. Annie read a lot, even the rubbishy tabloids.

Hal wasn't feeling at all fond of Willie. Sha had told him where she'd gone that night. 'Being busted's just like catching flu, you just gotta deal with it best way you can.'

'Willie's case it was more like pneumonia,' said George, then they let the subject drop, it was making them all uneasy, there were too many questions; too many things you just couldn't *know*.

The same grapevine that told about Willie also passed on another bit of news: one of Willie's father's companies had paid Kath a vast amount of money so they could bulldoze down her crummy shop.

Lucky Kath.

There were always things to be done at George's. Hal and George drove miles to saw and split a fallen macrocarpa on George's uncle's property and haul it home in trailer loads to stack for winter. It seemed to Hal a symbol of George's security that in the height of summer he took it for granted that winter would come and that his family would be together, in this same house, this winter. And the next.

Families. That was the secret, Hal told himself. Barbara was coming back for good. They would build a place at Piha, Hal would have a base and also flexibility. It could be the perfect solution. Strange how sometimes when things seemed to be falling apart they were in fact falling into place.

Then one of George's neighbours wanted to buy the bus. Hal felt his life was starting on a roll. Sometimes you just need the *inclination*, then you can sit back and watch it all pan out. Times like that you look back and see that decisions you made in the past — even the dubious ones like potting Willie — were all in a sense inevitable because they were contributing to the impetus of this big roll which all the time was on its way.

All Hal's gear was in the bus, but Annie said why not store it in the garage loft — he didn't even have to ask, he was rolling uphill and nothing could stop him. When he was clearing the bus he found the album that Kath had given him. Annie squeaked with pleasure when she saw the cover and dragged another copy from the back of the cupboard, saying Pita had got to it with a biro when he was two and she and George had been *so-oo* pissed off. All these years, never seen another copy going for sale.

'Keep it,' said Hal, 'it's yours.'

Annie kissed him on the cheek and said, 'I am such a fan of the way you play, you've no idea.'

'Even though you don't much approve of me as a human

being?' He wasn't meaning to sound petulant. He was interested by the thought that his music was something separate from him. That Hal Barber didn't need to be always on the line with a smile or a wisecrack, that he didn't need to keep *being* the singer, the keyboard man, because he was anyway, whether he liked it or not.

'I don't *dis*approve of you,' said Annie carefully. 'But I loved your music long before I met you.'

Holy shit, thought Hal. Of course he'd had things like that said to him plenty of times in the past, but they hadn't sunk in. Maybe he just hadn't believed them. It was as if Annie had lifted a heavy pack from his shoulders. *I'm there. I don't have to keep trying. My music knows how to handle itself; it's old enough to leave home.*

'That's it. Wonderful. Coffee time I think. Suzie, would you mind? Milk no sugar, Hal, right? Now that's exactly how we want to go but now we have it on video, so that's safety-pins as well as elastic. And we'll see you in exactly five hours. Right? Right. And don't worry, you're allowed to be a LITTLE excited.'

Said the man in his dealing-with-the-public voice. But Hal had no one to blame but himself. He didn't have to be there.

Then again in a sense he did, because wasn't Barbara's seeking him out just part of this inevitable upward roll?

Hal wished he'd had a few tokes on something, just to hold him down. He was *a little excited* after all. Maybe just nervous. The time seemed to be hurtling past, yet dragging. First there were the two old blokes who'd gone through the war together and stayed in touch till the early seventies when rheumatism kept one of them from replying to letters and the other gave up. He had been tucked in behind the screen with Hal until it was time for him to hobble out in front of the cameras. He'd looked ready for a seizure, but dogsbody Suzie was there to keep an eye on things and presumably had her resuscitation badge.

After that there was the heart-wrenching video clip of a girl whose father had given away her tortoise five years before. He had particular markings (the tortoise, that is) that she had painted on a sheet of paper and she hoped some viewer would recognise.

Hal watched this on a TV monitor while sitting at the piano in his little compartment, just as he had watched the old man being greeted by his old mate. It was happening just a few metres away but he was watching on screen.

After the tortoise the woman who loved Robert Redford made a small speech of her own saying, please, it wasn't a precedent for finding lost animals. Then there were a couple of screen items about people who were being sought. Then the man said, 'Remember this?' And an exterior video clip of a middle-aged woman with an embittered face half hidden by dark glasses came on screen and began talking about 'mah brawthuh in Paulmerstarn Nahth'.

So that when the real thing walked onto his little video screen the shock was just a tremor of that first major quake. He could see that the years had been hard on her, his clever sister, and that her sense of dress had frozen somewhere in the late sixties. And he was able to catch Suzie's eye and give her a reassuring smile that said, sure, he was Hal Barber and hip but he wasn't so shallow that he cared if his long-lost sister didn't match up.

Barbara sat down on the little sofa between her hosts and Hal noticed with relief that at least she wasn't chewing gum and that somewhere along the line she'd learnt not to sit with her knees apart.

He could hear her clearly and the absurdity of the whole thing — the organised artificiality of it — began finally to get to him. *His own sister* — so why didn't he just get up, push aside the screen and say, 'Hi!' Instead, along with half the country, he was passively being brought up to date on the fate of his family. Barbara had been a busy girl over there in California; she had tracked down their father who now lived in Hobart with a new wife and a second family and wished only for them all to be left in peace and ignorance, and she had tracked down Little Barry to a Golden Dawn rosebush in the Te Atatu Lawn Cemetery after his light plane nosedived into the Tararua Ranges in '81. And she had established that their mother had passed away at the Home of Compassion in Wellington in '79.

Once he'd adjusted to the accent, Hal felt a glow of warmth spreading through him. He was keeping one eye on Suzie who would give him the nod as to when he should start to play.

Barbara was talking about her 'brawthuh Henry'; were they close? 'Varry close. Yairs vairy.' The man was smiling encouragement. At some point, he understood, Henry had changed his name. What had he changed it to and why?

Barbara looked suddenly blank. Nerves. The man slipped smoothly into the silence. 'Hal,' he said. Barbara was ignoring him. She was craning her head around staring at the cameras and the camera operators with wild-eyed suspicion. The man made a small urgent hand signal and talked into the camera. 'Barbara's sister Hal, in fact grew up to be one of this country's . . .'

Suzie tapped Hal urgently on the arm and pointed to the keys. She was biting her lip in anxiety. Hal picked out the notes of 'Chattanooga Choo Choo', and they drowned out the man's next words. What had he said? *Most accomplished?. . . Favourite?. . . Most personable. . .?*

Oldest?

He began slowly then picked up speed the way they'd rehearsed. When he looked at the TV monitor the picture seemed shaky. The man and woman were standing, they were coaxing Barbara to move. She was pulling back stubbornly, showing the whites of her eyes. Hal's left hand joined his right, playing with a staccato tin-pan alley sound.

The screen was being removed. Barbara stood there between the man and the woman. Hal stood up. He'd forgotten how much shorter than him she was. Her eyes were bunched into slits as if she had trouble seeing him. The man gave Hal an urgent look and Hal stepped forward with his arms held ready to embrace this hard-faced little woman in the long girlish skirt and low-cut top.

But Barbara ducked beneath his approaching arm and hit the piano keys with her open palm like a toddler. She began to use both hands, crashing them down; rampaging sound, violent with discord. Hal looked at the man and woman — were they waiting for him to drag her away? He saw the look on the man's face was marginally euphoric; bastard was thinking, at Hal's expense, that this *could* just turn out to be the most rivetingly spontaneous TV moment of the decade.

Hal swung his eyes and saw the camera was on him, lapping

up his human-interest humiliation. He caught Barbara's arm and yanked her around. Her face was level with the second-to-top button of his shirt. She didn't look up. He put a hand beneath her chin and raised her face. 'Barbara,' he said. It seemed like a whisper. She stared back at him. Hal glanced at the camera, the black lens leered straight at them. Barbara turned to see what Hal was looking at. She leaned towards it, she smiled. 'Scraoutum,' she said.

A general breath of relief came from those standing around. Barbara had gotten hold of herself — a truly bizarre hiccup and now the show was back on the rails. What more could you ask?

'Sorry,' said the woman, leaning towards Barbara with an eager smile. 'Sorry, what was that?'

'Scraou-tum.' Barbara repeated slowly, patiently. Still none of them got it. They gave each other quick puzzled looks and frowns. Hal took a small step backwards, then another.

'Scraouwtum,' shouted Barbara. She reached with one hand and banged the piano keys. 'Scraouwtum, SCRAOUWTUM.'

Hal turned and headed for the door in long fast silent strides.

twenty-one

I sit at a round table in the airport bar sipping at brandy and ginger ale. I am surrounded by my friends. Well, *surrounded* is a bit strong, but Clive is here in a green shirt with white seagulls soaring around his torso, and Rose is here, looking surreptitiously at her watch because she has a meeting back in the city at 1.30. And Miriam and Tom drove all the way out to Clive's last night to wish me well and say sorry they couldn't make it. And Sha said she would be here, but isn't as yet.

There's still twenty minutes to go till boarding time. Clive had driven with such careful haste, even though we'd calculated margins for traffic jams and unforeseen emergencies. I was grateful that he shared, or at least understood, my unspoken fear of being *left on the ground*.

Clive is minding my records and books which, came the Grand Second Gear Closing Down Sale (household possessions included), I decided not to part with. I offered some to Sha but she turned up her nose. She accepted cutlery, glasses and the least reprehensible pieces of furniture for the bay-windowed room she'd found for herself in a Mt Eden student flat.

The night after the Grand Closing Down Sale, Sha and I threw a party. We got carried away and invited people we barely knew, including several of my regular customers. We refused to worry about things like smokers versus nonsmokers or straights versus bent ones; we issued invitations indiscriminately and people turned up and coped with what they found. Everybody seemed to have a good time. Kevin from the band turned up, and so did Cosmo. They kept shaking hands and thumping shoulders and calling each other *bro*. And Willie came, of course. But not Hal, who was last

170

seen on television being mauled by a bizarre American woman pretending to be his sister.

Strange that seeing him there on the screen — that first shot when they pulled away the curtain thing and there he was with his long ravaged face looking up from that vast concert piano — had seemed so fitting. I had thought, that's where he should've been all along — encased in black vinyl or safely trapped in cathode ray tubes. That's where all musicians belong — it would keep them from stumbling loose in the world and causing chaos.

Sha told me she hadn't watched. She said, 'He would've been hoping I was watching and feeling sorry for him, so I didn't.'

He rang me a few nights later. I'm still not sure what to make of his call. He didn't mention the *Reunion* programme, so neither did I. He said he'd been thinking a lot about the things we'd talked about, him and me. The future . . . his section at Piha . . . *life* . . . and he'd thought of other things he wanted to say to me. He intended coming back up to Auckland and how did I feel about that?

I had no answer. I simply said I was going away. And, saying it, I felt some regret but also much relief.

I haven't told Sha about his call. Telling her would serve no purpose.

The night of our party I went to bed with the man from the second-hand record shop, mainly so as not to be a bad sport. But also perhaps I was worried about what I'd been missing out on for a long time. We had, in accordance with the advertisements, safe sex. I proved to myself I was still in functioning order but it was light-years away from *Sid and Nancy*. Hal was the nearest I'd come to that in a long time, and in a strange way it was still there. I could rewind back to that scrappy lawn in the morning sunlight, to his wide mouth saying, 'I'll see you sometime,' and I knew for sure that my heart could beat up a storm. I was still *alive*.

And I guess that was how I wanted it. All I wanted. To be the fan who, one golden night, was given the scarf, or the kiss, or the ride on the roller-coaster, and to save that treasure like a snowstorm in perspex, so much more glorious than the real thing which always melts into sludge, turns heavy and grey, blocks your exits.

171

Clive wants to know if I still have the address of the woman in Canada. I tell him it's in my notebook. 'Give her my. . . fondest regards. You probably won't like her,' he says, 'but go if you get the chance.' I smile and nod but definitely don't intend to call on this Vicky in Montreal, even though I shall be in that city for a time visiting my brother and his Canadian wife, who I met when they came over for my father's funeral. Their three children must now be teenagers but are only known to me as three tiny crouching figures in an amateurish snapshot that came in a Christmas card several years ago.

Clive gathers up his glass and Rose's, and gets to his feet. I get to mine and try to push him back into his chair. 'I'll get them.'

'No, Kath. We're the ones farewelling you.'

'That's right,' said Rose. 'Besides you bought the last. . .'

'I want to,' I plead. I show them the last of my New Zealand money. 'I can't take it with me.'

Clive says, 'Kath, they have places at airports all over the world where you can change it.'

'Don't want to change it. I want to spend it.' And I do. Want that wild delight of dragging out notes and slapping them down on the counter. Buying ten-minute pleasures, nothing to show for it. My ancient leather handbag bulges with traveller's cheques and airline tickets, I'm frantic with irresponsibility. Easy come easy go.

They are no match for me, I grab the glasses and rush them to the bar counter. Dimly I have this extraordinary recollection of having seriously worried about taking this money. That somehow it would harm me — I would be *compromised*, for Godsake.

While I am being served, Sha and Willie come into the bar. The first that I know is the faces of the bar staff and an odd little flutter in the general drone of conversation. So I turn. I don't, at first, know it is Willie who trails behind Sha. He is dressed like a combat soldier, the ones we see eternally ploughing through swamps to sounds of Hendrix in TVietnam. His head is bald except for ridiculous little tufts of straw-like clown's hair and his face is painted up garish and desperate like an old whore. I look around at people at their tables. They stare, some are amused, others definitely aren't.

Clive joins me at the bar, he looks very happy. 'I'm getting drinks for your kinky friends,' he says. I drag out a five-dollar note and push it at him.

'I'm not broke,' he objects. 'However. . .' He gathers the note up.

Back at our table I carefully set down our three glasses. 'I see you're making a statement,' I tell Willie. I notice that underneath the make-up he's not all that happy.

'He'll grow into it,' says Sha. 'Won't you?'

Willie sighs and raises his black-pencil eyebrows.

'We don't want to steal your thunder,' Sha tells me. 'It just seemed like a good place to try it out.'

'I love it,' says Rose. She tells Willie, 'You're the best thing that's happened to me all week.'

Sha is waiting for my opinion but I'm still working on it. When I look at Willie half of me wants to laugh and the other half has that feeling you get when you're walking down the street at night and there are footsteps behind you keeping time with yours.

Sha burrows in her bag and passes out copies of a leaflet. A picture of this harlot soldier holding his guitar in firing position. *Willie de Struction and the Demented Saviours. April 16.*

'Lovely, dear,' I say. 'What a pity I won't be here.' I'm thinking that at least she won't miss me now that she's found an outlet for her creativity. And I'm thinking that the $3,000 I secretly deposited yesterday in her bank account is going to be blown on promoting this demented freak-show. And I'm thinking, what the hell, good luck to them both.

Clive returns with two small bottles of beer just as my boarding sign comes up on the monitor. 'That's it,' I say choking on my brandy. I start to stand up, I feel shaky. 'Don't come, please, please, finish your drinks, finish mine.' One by one I hug them all. I smudge Willie's lipstick. Rose says, 'Give my love to New York.' And Sha says, 'Tell them we're coming.' Meaning New Yorkers, for that's what I've been saying; *I'm going to see New York.* You say that and no one asks, what for. It's like saying *I'm going to see the centre of the Catherine wheel,* the fuse of the dynamite.

And I will. I'll go to New York, and to Montreal to see my brother who was always my favourite member of the family. And to Big Sur because of Richard Brautigan. But none of those places are what I'd call my *destination*. That bit I've told no one, not even Sha.

Least of all Sha.

The woman looks at me and at my photo. She smiles. She hands back the passport and all the other documentation that I've passed to her. I walk on through to what already seems like another country, occupied by strangers. I feel dizzy with excitement. The air fizzes into my lungs, I grin dementedly at incoming travellers. My secret fills me up like helium so that my new scarlet boots barely touch the floor as I walk. I say it to myself in my head, to help me believe.

I'm going to Graceland.